THE ARMOUR OF LIGHT

First Published in Great Britain 2015 by Mirador Publishing

Copyright © 2015 by Andrew Webb

First edition: 2015

A copy of this work is available through the British Library.

ISBN: 978-1-910530-70-2

Mirador Publishing
Mirador
Wearne Lane
Langport
Somerset
TA10 9HB

The Armour Of Light

By

Andrew Webb

Contents

Chapter 1

"I am the one and only!"

The Ford Sprinter van's radio boomed out the opening lines of the latest UK top ten hit as the Harrison family pulled into the driveway of their new home on the Surrey Hampshire border. Steve jumped from the driver's seat just before surveying the modern estate of bungalows in which he and his new family had just become new residents.

"Well, we haven't got much stuff so it should be an easy job," sighed Steve as his new wife Natalie put on a brave smile as she was hoping for a semi-detached house.

Her Ukrainian roots were still in her mind and heart as she was used to her own apartment with a balcony used for drying facilities. The young couple had only been married a few months since their wedding at Weybridge registry office and now the two of them and Alex, Natalie's son from her first marriage, had the bewildering task of settling down in the Surrey suburbs after leaving their uncertain past from Vinnitsa, their home town.

Steve Harrison was a local man with deep London roots as both his father and grandfather had served in the Metropolitan Police. "Eureka, there is a God!" as the main boiler finally burst into life after the new owner smiled after pressing the ignition switch on the Baxi heater cover for the fifth time. "The proof of the pudding is in the eating," he whispered to himself as he then awaited the home to heat up and get warm. After thirty minutes, Steve meticulously checked the radiators in every room then gave an appraisal as to how each room was offering its welfare to the family. He eventually came to the largest bedroom only to be met with a fierce defying chill that rejected heat at a stubborn cost. The radiator worked with a dull heat, but what was more enigmatic was that when Steve opened the window on that warm summer's morning, it seemed clear that it was warmer on the outside than it was on the inside.

"This is bloody strange," he said to his wife, who was leaning against the bedroom door, "we'll have to resort to plan B, the electric fires," he added as he swaggered off to the storage cupboard that was in the hallway. After twenty minutes of both electric fires burning away, Natalie returned only to discover that the room still had a stiff cold chill to it. "I just can't make it out," groaned Steve as he and his wife began to make the bed and hang up their clothes in the Scandinavian pine wardrobe.

"Perhaps the whole place has been unlived in for so long that the air has become stagnant," exclaimed Natalie, "and another thing, we have nothing to eat for lunch or dinner. There is a big Tesco at the large roundabout so what do you want?" she moaned in her thick fiery Slavic accent.

Alex was very quick to chime in, "Pizza!".

Steve quickly replied in a cutting tone, "anything that's junk food for you kids. Give you a pork chop and you just turn your nose up at it."

His mother exploded with a Slavic outburst with sympathy for her husband. Within five minutes both of them had downed tools and were in the 1.8 Volvo heading down the A30 to the usual mainstream life of nineties England.

"What do you think of it so far?" said Steve in an Eric Morecambe impressionist tone. Natalie did not see the joke. Instead she replied with a very unsure tone, "I hope you know what you are doing."

"What do you mean?" groaned Steve.

"I can't put my thoughts into words but there is a very strange atmosphere at that place."

"Nonsense!" snapped Steve.

"I'm not being stupid but I think we have made a big mistake coming here."

"Don't be stupid, Natalie. Can you please explain what you mean?"

"There's something about the place that make the hairs on my arms stand on end. It's in the air. There was this flat in Ukraine where a whole family died through poisonous gas. The mother and all her four children died when a gas water heater gave off poisonous fumes during the night. Months afterwards I had the chance to see the flat where is all happened and the biting cold made my skin crawl."

"Flaming 'eck, are you sure?" whined Steve.

"Steven, you must listen to me, I am talking to you!"

"That's enough of that," Steve snapped at his wife.

Alex was left to guard the new home and act as local security. As he leaned by his bedroom window with a glint of melancholy boredom in his eye, he gazed at the old garden perimeter wall which once belonged to the two old houses and a car mechanic's garage which once stood there before his new home was built. The surrounding area had a history of the esoteric which nobody in the area knew about. Over the years many of the old terraced houses in the surrounding streets had frequently changed ownership and the history of the district was lost by many of the locals in the fullness of time. Alex's very naive tender age didn't give any indication as to what had happened on this plot of land some twenty years before. His young unsuspecting mind, like his step-father, Steve, would accidentally stumble across a new home that would unfold a sinister mystery beyond their family's control.

There was a timid knock at the door as Alex arrived home from his new comprehensive school two miles from his new home as his mother very keenly rushed to answer it to hear of his daily results. The two of them had spent the previous evening meticulously doing and checking his mathematics home work.

"We did it!" Natalie shrieked as her son gleefully showed her his hard earned results.

"Oh, Steve will be pleased!" as this meant that Alex would be moved to a higher maths class just as he was in the Ukraine. His mother fastened her thick cardigan in response to the cold biting room temperature that all of them had to endure since moving in three weeks before. Natalie saved her emotions for her husband as this unsolvable issue had to be taken up yet again. She knew that this would not be easy as Steve had tried every domestic heating appliance to break this defying barrier.

"If we don't get this cold problem sorted out we'll go down with double pneumonia," he uttered to his wife upon his return from Heathrow later that evening. "Hah!" Natalie replied, "I've had that once before when the gas was cut off during Perestroika." She groaned. "Once is bad enough, I'm not going through all that again."

The couple congratulated themselves that evening as Natalie had been offered a job at the main Marks and Spencer department store. She had always been a natural mathematician which was contrary to her Soviet education and was more than happy to accept her post in the bureau de change.

"Well, I think its time for your bed now, Alex. Are you sure you've done all your homework as Steven is too tired to help you now?"

Despite the cold temperature of their bedrooms they relied on their own body warmth to heat up their beds.

It was gone 2.15 am and Steve began to twitch and turn in his restless sleep as his whole body rolled and convulsed from side to side, his mind repulsing to a vision far beyond his imagination. The black filthy bondage dungeon he was in was imprisoning young chain entangled victims, all groaning and convulsing with demented shivering. The walls were marked "666" in grotty white paint while screaming and howling could be heard from those begging to be released from a demonic trance while they crawled across the filthy ground with their hands and ankles bound with clanking chains. All Steve could do was watch, his eyes and mind transfixed until he couldn't take any more.

"What's the matter with you?" Natalie whispered as she held her husband. Steve stood up in bed, dripping in sweat. "My God, I've had the most bloody awful dream and I'm not telling you what happened." Natalie didn't reply but she had a very good idea what he meant as she'd had restless interrupted nights since their arrival. The two of them settled down between the sheets again, but Steve was quite convinced that his agile mind was trying to tell him something. He knew that his sixth sense was telling him that something was challenging his integrity. All Steve had to do was to take up the gauntlet.

Chapter 2

The M3 motorway that morning was very aggressive with every driver jostling for every space to get to work on time, dreading what their superiors would say on their late arrival. All the radio could offer was the news of Freddie Mercury's death and how many more companies had become insolvent in the past week.

"Hello, Mike, look mate, I can't stay long, but I think I'll be a few minutes late," said Steve to his colleague at the Heathrow cargo terminal. "My God, I feel bloody lousy. I'm sure it's something to do with our new home. Perhaps it's one of those sick buildings."

Later that morning Natalie was emptying her washing machine of all her white garments.

"Oh, bloody hell!" she blasphemed as she dug out two soaking wet tea bags from her entangled wet clothes. "Alex! I suppose this is another of your jokes."

"No, mum," he replied with a confused frown on his face .

There were brown blotches all over her husband's clothes. She thought nothing more of it until she realized that she hadn't made any tea until after she put the dirty washing in. "This is ridiculous," as she queried all this. As she hung all her laundry out she managed to grab the attention of Alan, their neighbour that lived opposite.

"Oh, I'm so glad I caught you but I'm Natalie Harrison from number four. Does your wife belong to a town women's guild?"

"What you should do is come along to the Conservative Club family evening that we have once a month at the end of Victoria Avenue. I can take you along there and get you proposed for membership."

"Oh yes, I know, I remember seeing an old photograph of that place in the nineteen fifties. I've been told that an old Edwardian house used to stand on this plot of land before our new bungalow was built." Alan frowned a bit and replied, "Oh yes, you mean the grange, an old doctor's surgery. That was demolished about the late eighties. I don't know exactly what happened but the GP then was suddenly taken into custody and banged up back in the 60's. Anyway, after that nobody wanted to buy the place as it was in great need of modernization. Jonathan Dean Developments bought this area of land and built Harley Meadows."

"So that's why we have this grotty old wall that runs along the end of our front garden," she chuckled.

"Yes, you could say that," groaned Alan, "as you can see we still have the old oak tree in the front garden and where your bay windows are used to be the front room, around the back was a car mechanic's garage."

Natalie thought this all sounded very eerie and vague.

That evening Natalie made a brave proposal to her husband. "Steve, I want to visit my mother this Easter as it's her seventieth birthday and I have this vision that this could be the last time I see her alive." Steve welcomed this idea as he always enjoyed his own space and privacy and as the two of them cleared the dining room table he looked up to Natalie and wearily groaned. "Oh, by the way, I've got to pop into the Halifax tomorrow lunchtime to hand in a copy of the endowment policy for the Legal and General."

The following afternoon Steve took a late lunch from his office and went for a stroll about the shopping complex in nearby Staines . He noticed there was a Virgin megastore at the far end and, after handing over his documents at the Halifax, was beckoned inside to choose a video to interest and entertain his mind from the endless evening chores that Natalie gave him. After surveying the comedy section several times his attention was drawn to the history department . "Ah, that looks handsome," he uttered in his Cockney accent as his eyes caught the Third Reich videos that were neatly bunched together on the lower shelf. 'Occult History: Himmler the Mystic' was picked off the shelf by Steve's fickle finger. He had always been a keen historian of all the wars, especially German history. The back of the box described the video as an autobiography and without any second thought he made his way to the scruffy, spiky haired assistant behind the cash register and paid by debit card. "This should make excellent viewing while I'm on my tod," grinned Steve, as he knew that his dominant wife always deplored the German war machine that destroyed her country during the Great War.

That evening Steve gleefully cooked his own evening dinner of pork and all the trimmings as Natalie and Alex went to his usual football training. Prior to cutting his first mouthful he peeled off the crisp plastic wrapping, carefully took the cassette from its new unmarked box and went through the ritual of playing it on his well-used VCR. The television screen burst into life with sharp snare drum beats as mystic icons of semi-naked Viking figures with swords and black swastikas intermittently appeared down the right hand side of the screen, followed by old German aristocratic photographs from the turn of the century. Steve soon got the idea that this documentary was not necessarily about Himmler, but about the Occult of the Third Reich and Nazi Party, which portrayed a very demonic type of spiritualism. The dialogue was very complicated and complex to understand as it covered esoteric societies, psychic mediums and communication with the Aryan Gods, Saxon Kings and Nordic race soul. "Bloody hell," Steve whispered in disbelief as the video moved onto 'Himmler's Black Order' and how he was guided and advised by Karl Maria Wiligut, a Nazi occultist that he enrolled into the SS and made a full Brigadier, proclaiming that he was in a long line of mystic teachers reaching back to prehistoric times. Steve quite naturally became blinded with science and resorted to turning up the volume, thinking that its very in-depth dialogue would become more comprehensible.

"My God, this really is hard going," groaned Steve as he wearily brushed back his hair with his sweaty hands. When it had finished playing he hid it at the back of his bookcase, knowing that his wife would throw it out if she discovered it. His enquiring mind had got the better of him. This mystifying archive documentary had beckoned him to play it again and again during his wife's absence until its message came clearer to him. Unbeknown to Steve, he was also attracting a power beyond his control. By persistently playing this occult video he was sending strong invitation messages to the spirit world that scarred the ground that his home was built on.

Chapter 3

"Well, if that's the lot I'll chuck your bags in the car then," quipped Steve as Natalie and Alex made their last minute farewells to their next door neighbours. Natalie was very pleased as she had booked a very good economy deal with BA for a return fare for less than £300.00. She had spent many weekends making all the preparations, buying the different types of medicine that could not be bought in the Ukraine plus US dollars as her mother was struggling on her old Soviet pension. Her vacation for six weeks would give her husband a generous amount of free time to do whatever he wanted, when he wanted and how he wanted. The only drawback would be the cooking, washing, ironing and all the mundane domestic chores. Apart from all this Steve was as free as a bird for weeks. He was now let off the lead.

With his 1.8 Volvo parked at Hatton Cross tube station, he quickly boarded the Piccadilly line to Edgware Road where his old school friend Jim and his girlfriend Dana lived in a very old Victorian basement flat in Old Marylebone Road, London, to spend the day and night in Leicester Square. The bars were full of typical young people that had just finished work, all making the most of their single life. "Well, Jim, I've got rid of the old woman for a month, it'll be just like the good old days when we were single back in the eighties."

"Yeah, sure, with all the music at the Empire, Rick Astley and all that," slurred Jim as Steve grinned with mutual sympathy. Trafalgar Square's traffic gave a monstrous noise of urban barrage as taxis and every conceivable form of four wheeled transport travelled around Nelson's column in a clockwise direction.

"All this shit reminds you of the Arc de Triomph. Could be our version of it, I suppose," slurred Steve as he looked at his mate, expecting an equally cynical remark. Jim breathed in hard, smacked his lips and replied, "Yeah, I see what you mean." All this was very nostalgic for both of them as they had given up their single lives for the commitment of relationships and even more so the commitment of home ownership. The two rather intoxicated men shook hands and departed at Hyde Park corner as Steve put his left foot on the underground escalator to begin his journey back to his lifeless silent home in Surrey.

As he put his key into the lock and pushed open the door he picked up the letters awaiting him on the door mat and tossed them into the bedroom next to the hallway. The whole atmosphere was one of total stony silence. Not a pin drop could be heard. After making himself a small milky cup of instant coffee he wandered into the lounge and sprawled over the sofa before preparing himself for bed. He felt quite sure that Natalie and Alex had made it safe and sound to Vinnitsa as they had left a message on the telephone answering machine. It was now 1.15 am.

"Come on, Harrison, get a grip, boy, time you got yourself to bed," he muttered to himself as he staggered to their bedroom and flicked on the lights. Four seconds later the light went out in a controlled manner as though a decision had been made by something. "The bulb's obviously gone," uttered Steve with slight irritation and, after taking one from the storage cupboard, he screwed it into the socket. There was still no light. "Right! Try the fuse." The fuse was as sound as a pound. "Well, this really is bloody weird, Steve my boy," as he could see himself having to pay an over-zealous electrician's bill to resolve this matter. After cleaning his teeth he flopped onto the bed and crawled under the duvet, falling asleep after ten minutes.

It was 7.15 in the morning and Steve's eyes gradually opened. The lights were on and sure enough the brightness of the bulb made him get out of bed to turn it off. "What the bloody hell's going on, man?" he thought. Perhaps there was a loose connection or something? An hour later Steve tried the lights again and after four seconds they cut out. After telephoning his father to seek advice he put on his brown leather jacket and set off to do his shopping.

That evening the television remained on as it boomed out various documentaries, weekly news, game shows and dramas. It was a typical Saturday evening and Steve wandered from room to room wondering what to do with himself. He was alone, surrounded by the cold silence that reminded him of his old bachelor days, as his greasy body and groin felt that the rest of the evening should be spent having a steaming hot bath with all the luxury shampoos and toiletries that go with it. Imperial leather soap, Harvey Nichols shampoo and Avon bubble bath. The full works. All this should boost his mind to a euphoric high to end the day. As the tall but sturdy thirty six year old belted out Tom Jones songs of the sixties, he spent a good hour in the bath. "What's new pussy cat, wow, wow, wow!", yodeling all the famous choruses from the Welsh singer's repertoire. Feeling fresh and invigorated he stepped across the hallway and navigated his hand around the bedroom doorway to the light switch.

Click on went the light. "Good!" he exclaimed.

"Oh blast, not again!" as the light went out as pitch black darkness engulfed the room. After midnight the weary man slid into bed and surveyed the room around him. The digital clock reading 12.47, the portrait picture of the King Charles

Bridge in Prague on the wall and the ornaments on the bedside dresser. Steve lay there gazing at the wall at the end of his bedroom with innocent interest.

"Bloody hell! My God! Bloody hell!" he stuttered as a white cloud of smoke began to billow from the centre of the wall. With his body totally dumb struck with shock and devastated fear, the cloud made its way sweeping across the room towards him with a swishing ray-like tail at its rear.

Steve began to convulse with utter dismay as it stopped over him as it turned into a black smoky colour like fumes from an incinerator. He just laid there, his body pumping out sweat as the bed sheets soaked up the dampness . This could only mean one thing . All the questions and queries that had mystified the whole family for months could now be answered. Their home was haunted.

As he regained his courage he stared at the entity and growled in an authoritarian tone.

"In the name of God I command you to get out!!!"

The cloud stayed there for a full five minutes, then it gradually disappeared. The atmosphere of the room sounded strange, as if it had shrunk in size. Although Steve lay there petrified by this experience, he felt a sense of gladness that the strange secret of their home had revealed itself. After a few hours he managed to relax and fall asleep until he awoke five hours later to find that the bedroom lights had restored themselves to normal and were shining brightly again. What Steve didn't realize that the demon was waiting for him to return to the bungalow. By playing with the electric lights it had prepared and warned him of its intention to make its appearance and materialize.

Chapter 4

"Well, I'd better tell ya, something's happened." Steve decided to break the silence at his parents' Sunday lunch table. He gave an accurate account of what had happened the night before.

"Good heavens!" his mother gasped in total surprise. His father reacted in a not too surprised response. "Well, if that had happened to me I would have fainted. Phew!" added his mother. His father asked what he had been doing to cause this and Steve admitted that he had persistently played a very intense occultist Nazi video. "Well, I'm not surprised you've got troubles. You've been sending out invitation messages to spirits and God knows what. I think that you should contact your local Church of England as they are known for carrying out exorcisms," advised his father. "They have St Michael's Church of England on the London Road. I'll see about writing to them." The rest of the day was spent discussing everything that happened that night.

Ring, ring! The telephone rang from the living room late that Wednesday evening.

"Hello, this is Bruce Webster from St Michael's. I've received your letter about your home problem. When is the best time I can call round?"

"Oh great, this sounds really promising. At long last I can get this place sorted out once and for all," thought Steve.

"Any time next week, Bruce, as long at its after seven in the evening."

"OK, well how about next Tuesday?"

"That's fine with me," Steve gladly replied. "OK, that's in my book, I'll see you Tuesday about eight o'clock then."

As soon as Steve hung up, his mind went into a spin as to what Bruce would do. Would he come armed with the cross and garlic just like those films he had seen on late night television as a young child? How would he tackle this problem? As Steve sat there on the sofa he became excited but at the same time he knew that he would have to keep the whole thing secret from his wife.

The following morning he shared his news with his colleagues at work. Some were interested and thrilled as to what would happen next. Others became wary that he was some sort of freak, possibly with a history of mental illness, but the accounts manager, Tony, made a huge joke about the whole thing.

Buzzzzzz

"Hello, Bruce, do come on in and I'll take your coat from you," Steve welcomed Bruce on that cold evening, as he led him into the lounge. Bruce looked like a typical church minister, short and dumpy with a short goatee beard and bald head with just short hair on the sides.

"Would you like tea or coffee?"

"Oh, tea please, Steve."

Steve looked at Bruce, somewhat confused, as all that Bruce had brought with him was a rather thick and tatty bible. After fifteen minutes of them sitting on the sofa, Steve had finished explaining the whole scenario.

"Do you believe me?" Bruce was asked.

"I take this very seriously," he replied.

Steve was expecting a much more helpful answer than this. At the end of the meeting Bruce only said that he would go away and pray for Steve and return in a week's time. He was very disappointed with this proposal.

Nothing else happened for several days. Steve got into bed later on that week and fell asleep after a hard day's work at Heathrow. As he lay on his side he fell into a mediocre sleep.

Bang! *Shweeeeeep*!

Steve woke up in a state of shock as he hadn't a clue what was happening, as he felt something crash across his legs in bed. The whole bedspread felt as though it was about to be pulled off him. After about two seconds he gradually opened his eyes. To his horror and amazement he saw a white flickering figure of a most ugly old man with chattering teeth wearing a checked night shirt, his head moving from side to side. This brief glimpse lasted about five seconds until it suddenly disappeared with a flash.

"Bloody hell, this really is for real," Steve whispered under his breath as his whole body pumped out cold sweat, making the whole bed damp and uncomfortable.

Bruce returned a week later, Steve expecting him to solve the problem by carrying out a time of prayer in every room and to do some sort of ritual to put an end to these unwanted visitations. As his rather boring guest took off his coat, Steve looked at Bruce with eager anticipation. Bruce sat on the sofa, his head buried deep into his bible as he flicked through to find chosen verses in the New Testament.

"I have a few words of scripture for you, Stephen, which should help you." Steve frowned as though he was expecting something better and more dramatic.

"For God so loved the world that he gave his only …"

"Oh, bloody hell," thought Steve as his rather grey guest droned and rattled on in a rather matter or fact tone. He felt that he had to be polite to Bruce as he wasn't paying him anything.

"My church is very low on numbers and I would like to see you come along on Sunday," he added. "We've not quite reached the happy clappy stage yet but we like families and people of your age."

"Hmmm, how most congenial of you," he thought.

"Bruce, there is one thing I've got to tell you. Since you last came there has been another bad incident and I want to know if there is anything you can do? It's not got any better and I need serious help."

Bruce glanced up with an unsympathetic glance.

"Well, they're not doing anything to harm you."

Steve leaped to his feet and exploded at him.

"You don't seem to understand! What I've got in my home comes from down there!" He stabbed a very forthright finger to the carpet. "You church-going people are only interested in looking on the bright side of life and dancing in the aisles. You ought to pay attention to helping God fight his enemy, Satan, because that's what I've got in my home!"

The two men stared angrily at each other for several seconds. Bruce broke the silence.

"I see you're very angry."

"Yes, I am," replied Steve in a very stony, cold voice.

Bruce rose and stood up, pulled on his coat and made his way for the door. Before he left he half turned around and gave a "huh" of contempt before closing the door behind him. The two men never met again.

The following morning Steve dialed directory enquiries for St Paul's Church of England on the other side of town. He was lucky enough to be put through to Rev Mark Chester, who showed much more concern and decided to ring him back.

"I think you need a specialist to sort out this problem," he advised and wished him the best of luck.

That night was one of those thick muggy hot nights that went with English weather. Steve lay there tossing and turning all over the bed, wondering how his wife was getting on in Vinnitsa. He knew he had to get an answer to this problem or how would he explain this to Natalie, as not only was this a threat to the whole family but totally embarrassing as well. Something was drawing on his mind as if some external power held the reins over his thoughts. He gradually awoke and slowly opened his eyes to focus what was around him.

"What the hell!" he exclaimed in his mind.

There by the bedroom door stood a totally black figure about six feet tall wearing a long black cloak with a pointed head and a long pointed nose. The figure was all black from head to toe except for its eyes that were white slits and by the outline of its body, Steve could see that its arms were folded. As he lay there curled up in bed, the black figure stared at him for several moments.

"Is this thing going to be here all night gawping at me or what?" he thought as he decided to shut his eyes and have a doze until it went. Ten minutes later he opened them again. To his astonishment the figure was still there, staring at him with no compromise. Steve took stock of himself and sat up in bed, propping himself up with his right arm. The figure hesitated, turned around and then silently disappeared through the wall.

"It's gone," he wheezed in relief.

"That's the third one we've had."

Who would believe him of this paranormal activity? How could he explain all this to his wife?

The following morning was spent at Steve's office at Colnbrook, Heathrow. His colleagues had become amused but also not amused at his home troubles, as the company he worked for had had a very bad record of employing staff of a social misfit nature, loners and paranoid people. He certainly did not want to follow suit. If he got himself a reputation of being a weirdo this would obviously bar his way for promotion and earning better money, which he needed quickly. He felt himself trapped with this traumatic absurd problem. Who would believe all this ? Was he really mad or had some sort of mental illness? This could get him the sack. They might think he was on drugs. One thing could lead to another. He started to get worried and bothered. There was a bad recession on and he certainly didn't want to lose his job. Steve had to find the right man that could help. The other two men had let him down.

That lunchtime Steve met his mother in Ashford High Street. Jean was very concerned about his welfare.

"What about the paranormal?" she asked in her typical London nagging voice.

"It's got worse, mum," he replied in a very weary tone.

"I've had a black figure wearing a long black cloak this time."

"Oh my God, no," she moaned loudly. Then she added, "Look, I'll ask around at the local Townswomen's Guild as we've had all sorts of speakers with all sorts of topics and problems," she advised.

"Oh yes, I remember," smirked Steve.

"Last time you had Val Messender giving a talk on gender dysphoria."

His mother just grinned and grimaced.

"Now look, I'll be in touch."

Sure enough Jean rang back the following Friday. "We had the Reverend David Holmwood come to lecture on your problem a few years ago and I've got his number."

Steve rang and an elderly man answered the telephone. The man was very sympathetic but told him that David Holmwood was on a mission trip to South America.

"I'll take your number and he will get back to you, which won't be for another month."

"That's too late. Natalie will be back in two weeks," thought Steve. He felt like Walt Disney's magician's apprentice and hadn't a clue on how to reverse things.

Chapter 5

The traffic tunnel from terminal one made an amplified echo as Steve collected Natalie and Alex from the airport arrival lounge. She gave a never ending account of her visit to her somewhat grumpy husband. Steve listened with a very pensive ear, also thinking.

"Oh yeah, well wait until you hear what's been going on while you've been away."

As the two unpacked their luggage in their bedroom, Natalie questioned why their home had got much colder. Steve had a very good answer.

"It's that boiler again. It's not very effective, dear. It's a water heater really, not up to heating eight radiators."

Steve was lucky enough that his wife would believe the excuse as she proposed that both of them should sleep on the sofa bed in the lounge, which was a bit warmer and cosier.

After they had finished their borge broth and Ukrainian salad, the two got into bed and by 11.30 were fast asleep. By early morning Steve woke up bursting to use the toilet and, to his utter dismay, saw many transparent black figures gliding across the end of the room from left to right and into the kitchen. One figure appeared through the far end wall and swept across the room towards Steve and then did a right turn though the wall that led to Alex's bedroom. They made absolutely no noise, just many comings and goings from two directions like Clapham Junction. After clenching his bladder he slipped out of bed, made his way to the door and tiptoed his way to the toilet. By the time he returned Natalie was curled up under the sheets and sobbing. Steve just held her in his arms and she just said in a voice of total surrender, "You don't have to explain, I've seen it all." He was relieved as he was not stuck with the job telling his wife of what had happened in her absence. All he had to do was embrace her and hold her until daybreak. For the next two weeks the two of them slept in the lounge as their bedroom was too cold for any use.

Over the next few days Steve began to investigate as to why all this paranormal mayhem had erupted in his home as he was very suspicious that all this was caused by what had stood on the plot of ground before his bungalow was built. A few evenings later he arrived home from work, parked up the car and shot across the road like a trooper avoiding sniper fire to Edward House, the flats opposite. There he had become acquainted with a middle aged chap, Andy Bunn, whom he nicknamed "Sticky Bun". Andy had lived there since 1981 and seemed the most likely person to give the best answer.

"Andy, can you tell me what stood on that plot of ground before my home was built because I've had God knows what come through my bloody walls in the last six weeks?"

Andy very calmly replied in a very composed voice, "There was an old garage that stood there back in the sixties and seventies that a gang used for Ouija board sessions and things like that. I didn't want to tell you this as I didn't want you to get worried and afraid. I have heard from the previous owners that strange things have been seen there."

That afternoon at the office was a very silent one. The telephone calls were very infrequent and everyone was casually chatting across the desks. Suddenly the receptionist turned around on her office swivel chair and shouted.

"Steve, it's David Holmwood!"

"What?" he replied in a slightly irritated tone, "oh yes,

great," as he suddenly realized who the caller was. The man with all the answers.

"Hello, Steve," a clear and well-spoken man introduced himself down the telephone. "I've a message to call you." Steve explained all that had happened and Holmwood replied, "Oh, why do those blasted people have to dig up the sewers and release all mayhem? Now look, I've just returned from Venezuela and I've got your phone number and I'm very heavily booked up at the moment so I'll have to call back in the near future ." Steve felt let down again, but he felt that this was his only hope.

Another week went by and he and his wife still continued to sleep in the lounge. They felt safe and warmer there but they never entered their bedroom as it had such a deathly cold presence to it. Again, Steve called Holmwood and received a promising reply. "Don't worry, I've not forgotten you. Are you free this Friday evening?"

"Yes, of course," he replied with a feeling of 'this is now or never' on his mind.

They both agreed to 7.00 pm and Holmwood finished by saying.

"Don't sleep in that bedroom until I get there and keep that door shut."

"That goes without saying," thought Steve.

As soon as he put the telephone down he noticed that half the office had gone quiet and everyone was looking in his direction, some of them having this slightly stony expression on their faces.

Steve got home that Friday evening and Natalie had arranged welcome refreshments for their guests. They both sat on the sofa in complete silence until 7.00 pm.

The phone rang.

"We are running a bit late but we will be with you."

"OK, David, we'll be waiting."

Finally at 7.20 there was a buzz at the door and in stepped an elderly man in his sixties dressed in full Baptist church ministerial uniform, carrying a bible and a thick wad of papers and a brief case. "He looks very similar to Jessie Yates from Stars on Sunday,", thought Steve with a slight smirk on his face. After everyone was seated in the lounge, Natalie brought in the tea and biscuits, only for them to be refused by David. The first thing he did was to start surveying the room looking for anything that would be an invitation message to spirits.

"I see you have many video cassettes on the Third Reich. There is Adolf Eichmann, Reynhard Heydrich, Himmler and all sorts. All these are acting like a magnet to the other side," he explained.

"You need to throw them all out, not just one or two, to break the demonic hold on your home."

He then pointed his pen to a small hieroglyphic papyrus picture hanging in the dining room area. The picture was of an Egyptian woman wearing traditional head dress, kneeling down with her hands out in a welcoming manner with various icons on the left hand side.

"Do you know what this means?" asked Holmwood.

"No, not at all," Steve replied.

"Can I ask why you bought it?"

"I just thought it looked good," he replied, becoming a bit defensive in his tone.

"Well, it's of an Egyptian woman trying to contact her dead husband."

"Blimey!" exclaimed Steve.

"This is also an invitation to spirits."

Holmwood explained some further facts. "As you know by now, the Nazis were great followers of the Occult, Himmler being the main one with all his mystic icons and his castle of Wevelsburg that was the centre of SS spiritualism." Steve also added that before his home was built stood an old garage and doctor's surgery that was used for an occult gang's operation centre and to carry out Satanic rituals.

"This land is spiritually scarred," said Holmwood. "Many sprits have been called to this area of land and can't find their way back. They are stuck in a dimension between heaven and hell. You see, Steve, in the spirit world dark attracts dark and like attracts like. All your Nazi paraphernalia has attracted dark spirits."

"Yes," replied Steve, "a lot of the ghosts I have seen have been semi-opaque black. There has been a black figure that I have seen twice that wears a cloak and has a long pointed nose that always stands by the bedroom door."

"That is an angelic being," replied Holmwood. "That is a demonic sign that something rather bad has happened here and so they have been called here. They usually stand with their arms crossed with a tutting posture. They can also grow in size and have white slits for eyes. They are not a ghost but a demonic spirit."

Steve was absolutely mesmerized and spellbound by what he heard. All of this was out of this world and would make massive material for conversation. Incredible and unbelievable. After forty minutes of hearing his tales of woe, Rev Holmwood decided that the time had come to begin the exorcism.

"I want to begin as I usually do by praying for the armour of light. When I do this I pray that the Lord God will provide us with an invisible barrier of light that surrounds our whole body from head to foot. No spirit or entity can touch or push us in any way so we are totally protected. We must also open all the windows in every room so that when the spirits are ejected they can escape through an open window. If there is no other way for them to escape, they have been known to smash windows to find an escape route."

Holmwood said a short prayer asking for the whole home to be cleansed of all demonic evil and for all the spirits to leave. They prayed in every room, opening every window, asking every spirit to look to the light. Steve was expecting some dramatic reaction as they moved from the lounge to the kitchen, then to the bathroom and hallway until they came to the smallest bedroom. This was the high spot of the evening. "The bedrooms are the worst areas where we get all the problems," said Steve in a relieved tone of voice. "They have stayed untouched and un-entered over the past few weeks." Holmwood gripped the door knob firmly and gave the door a very strong push. A harsh, deathly, cold breeze came from the pitch black room. As the two of them entered one behind the other, Steve suddenly yelled, "Aaaaarrrrrgggggg! Something had just gone past me at walking speed that felt like massive voltage electricity!" Holmwood replied, "I felt it as well and I saw a young girl in a long Victorian dress make her way through that internal wall."

"I've just felt four fingers on my shoulder," said Steve. They opened the window and prayed for five minutes. They then left and made their way to the main big bedroom. As they stood by the doorway, their hearts began to pound as they realized that anything could be in the next room. Suddenly, Holmwood once again grabbed the door handle and tried with his full strength to open it.

"It just won't turn but it feels that something the other side is holding it fast and stopping it from turning." Steve quickly chimed in, "All right, Dave, give it here and I'll sort it out." He thought of something that usually made him angry to give him the aggressive energy that he needed. As he gritted his teeth he gave an enormous roar and turned the knob slowly, then tried to push the door open until Holmwood stepped forward and pushed against the door with all his might. Between them they gradually pushed open the door as though

25

it had a ton of iron behind it. As the two of them looked into the room, Holmwood made the first step only to cry out, "I can't go in! It's pushing me back. I'll have to go down on my hands and knees to crawl in." As both of them made their way to the end of the bed they had a long struggle to stand on their feet again. He saw by the wardrobe the angelic being wearing its usual black gown with white slits in its head. It looked two dimensional.

Holmwood stood up with Steve's aid and shouted with his right finger pointing, his arm fully stretched, "In the blood of the Lord God I command you to leave this family's home. You are the servants of Satan and in the name of God I command you to be banished from this home." The figure remained and did not move. It was defiant as Steve gripped Holmwood's shoulder.

"In the blood of Christ I command you to go."

Suddenly out of the darkness of the room was hurled their large brass alarm clock.

"Aarrgghh, damn blighter!" yelled Steve as it struck him in the chest. Holmwood, in his defiance to this act, shouted in tongues, "In the name of God I command you to leave, GO!" The angelic being turned around and disappeared through the wall with a loud windy blowing noise. Holmwood was not convinced that the room was rid of its spirits. He gave a prayer in English followed by the same in tongues.

Swish, bang, smash like the noise of an underground train arriving at its station.

"It's gone, I felt a spiritual reaction," said Holmwood.

"It's a shame I wasn't able to open the windows," said Steve.

"Now we've got some clearing up to do."

It was 12.15 as the last nail was hammered home to repair the broken window with board and masking tape.

"If you have any more trouble then feel free to give me a

call. They have a very bad habit of coming back," Holmwood warned as the two of them shook hands as Natalie, who was very emotionally shaken by the whole evening's events, showed him the way to the front door so that he could be given a warm thank you and seen off the premises.

"Oh, just before you go, I would like to give a donation to your church, David, for all the help and attention you have given tonight."

Natalie fetched a small white envelope from the desk containing forty pounds and offered It to Rev Holmwood, thinking it would be gladly received.

To her dismay, Holmwood stood there with his hands straight by his sides and did not move as though he was rooted to the ground, his face all very stony faced as though he was offended by such a gesture. He replied in a bitterly offended tone.

"I do not get paid for my work and I do not accept any donations for any churches. What I suggest you do is buy something spiritually pleasant for your home in the near future."

Natalie stood there totally confused as, in her culture from eastern Europe, all cash donations are well received by everybody.

Upon leaving their home, Holmwood paused for a second in front of Natalie and made a frigid angry face at her, giving a rather bad end to the evening.

The air in the flat seemed a lot fresher and lighter as the two of them settled down to sleep for the night after a rather traumatic experience.

"Well, that's that all gone, I can feel it," sighed Natalie.

"Only time can tell," replied Steve, somewhat tongue in cheek.

Chapter 6

It had been three weeks at least since their home had been released from its esoteric grip. The atmosphere in their home had changed a lot as the air felt more like pure oxygen than the oppressive, stuffy, un-breathable matter they had endured since their arrival. Natalie had decided to make some re-arrangements to the flat to make a statement that they were making a new beginning to their modest bungalow. They all noticed how much warmer their home was and had lost its stubborn chilly bite and the headaches they had to endure became far less frequent. They firmly believed they had begun a new life of peace and family harmony without the unwelcome intrusions which they had the courage to tolerate. In the bedroom Natalie had re-arranged all the furniture so that the bed was positioned at the opposite wall with the headboard close to the doorway.

The memories of that evening had stayed in Steve's mind. The two big questions that haunted him were why and how should this have to happen to them. One lunch time he went to his local library to read up on the topic of the paranormal. There was one large book complete with photographs that discussed poltergeists (noisy ghosts), but what was more interesting was that most ghosts were not white glowing figures but were semi-opaque black. Another common factor mentioned was ghosts of young children holding hands with the eldest one standing in the middle. Ghosts like to turn on appliances and set off smoke alarms etc. even though they don't have any batteries in them. Also ornaments and small items are arranged in a small childish pattern, stones are thrown at glass windows from the outside and the slaughter of small animals are common factors of paranormal activity.

Natalie had made friends with an elderly Polish lady, Josephine, who she had met at the local launderette while drying her duvet covers.

"Could you look after our cat, Jinga, for seventeen days while we are in Singapore?" was the request of this tall spectacled lady. So the family were handed the Siamese cat, which took to them very well. It just curled up on the sofa with its chin on its paws and purred loudly every time it was stroked. It seemed perfect, quite happy and content at home until the second night when its was having its coat grooming session with its eyes fixed on the television, when suddenly it jumped backwards with a sharp flinch as its eyes glided from one side of the room to the other. Its coat bristled, at the same time giving a very distinctive and confident howl. Natalie had a very good idea why the cat had done this. She could see something that could only be seen by a cat or dog but not by a human. It obviously came through an outer wall and made its way across the lounge and through the other wall into Alex's bedroom.

"Oh no, oh bloody hell no!" yelped Steve. It reminded him of the famous last saying, "Just when you thought its was safe to go back in the water."

Jinga the cat trotted over to the other side of the wall and gave a very inquisitive sniff.

"What's the matter with the puss?" asked Natalie. The cat started meowing very loudly as it was clearly upset by something. Its coat took on a very strange spiky appearance as its eyes became glued to the wall.

"I think its seen something we haven't, but never mind, carry on as though nothing has happened," said Steve in a rather cheesed off tone. The cat eventually settled and returned to the sofa but Natalie and her husband were far from relaxed. They continued to watch the television until the end of the news at 10.30 and began to get themselves ready for bed. That night Steve slept very badly with his body twisting and turning, his mind drifting in and out of consciousness until it made a submitting decision to wake up. He opened his eyes and there before him about two feet away was the same black angelic being staring down at him. It had the same white slits for eyes and a large beak for a nose that engulfed most of its face. It was totally black like a Kodak negative. Steve stared back at it with a most unaccommodating stare.

"Go now, go!" snapped Steve and then suddenly it turned sideways and glided straight through the wall.

"This is for real. This is dual, I know it is. This is what this thing wants," he thought.

He felt totally confused and disappointed as he felt that this problem should have gone. Holmwood had told him that these spirits have a bad habit of returning and that he had to try again and again to get rid of them. Perhaps they would never go and he and his family had to learn to live with them. Maybe another solution should be used as he had seen in the local paper that spiritualist mediums were advertising their services to call them away and to leave the home in peace. The one advert that did catch his eye was clearly headed "William Psychic". Steve pondered over this for a few minutes until he gingerly picked up the receiver and dialled the number. A strange sounding woman answered the telephone, took Steve's address and number and told him that her husband would contact him when he returned home. He knew that these psychic people were really spiritualists that were in touch with the spirit world and he believed that this would tell him the answer to ridding their home of these unwanted entities.

Later that evening, the phone rang and a rather warm

sounding gentleman announced himself and after he explained his technique, asked for Steve's date of birth and fixed an appointment for the following Tuesday at 8.30 pm. He was very fortunate that his wife was working that evening as she would have objected to having this man in their home.

The door buzzer went at 8.37 and a tall man with grey hair carrying a case stepped into the home of the Harrisons. William started by telling a lot about himself and how he had lived in the area for many years and then he started studying all the lines and curves on Steve's hands and gave a very patchy history of his life, which he found very amusing as this sounded like anybody's life. He predicted a very vague future but at the end of the session Steve said hesitantly.

"There has been one problem that I've had with this place since we moved in a while ago."

"Haunting," replied William, looking him right in the eye with a very knowing expression on his face.

"Yes," he replied.

William took over. "I know about this estate and what stood here before this place was built. I also know you've got an old man with chattering teeth here."

Steve was absolutely stunned with what he had heard. How could William know about this as he had not been told anything about this strictly confidential information.

"When I entered your hallway I felt a very strong oppressive spiritual presence. I remember when an old car mechanic's garage stood here on this very spot and next to it was a doctor's surgery called the Grange. A gang carried out occult meetings in the garage and slaughtered animals in Satanic rituals, but they were tipped off to the Police by neighbours and were sent to prison about 1970."

"My God, that's amazing," he thought, but it seemed that William only knew about contacting spirits but didn't know anything about getting rid of them. Although the meeting had been a very Interesting one, he felt that it had knocked the issue sideways. Furthermore, he thought that he had angered the spirits that would get their revenge against him.

Later that evening, Steve collected Natalie from her job and both of them were in jubilant mood. She was totally unaware of what had happened and looking forward to putting her feet up and a hot drink, as well as pouring her heart out to her husband about the day's events and how this and that could be a lot better. By midnight both of them had finished brushing their teeth and were both in bed.

"Alex told me last night that something heavy sat on his bed last night and thumped him on his shoulder," said Natalie in a very pensive tone.

"Oh yeah," groaned Steve, "Well, it least he hasn't had a serious accident like being knocked down or had petrol thrown over him or something."

"You always have an answer for everything," Natalie replied in her thick Slavic accent. "You very foxy like Tony Blair," she said. But Steve also knew that she could be very shrewd, to say the least. As time passed by, the silence of the night drifted Natalie off to sleep, but Steve felt as though he had his guard up about something. He was not at ease as his mind began searching for a way to sort out his future. As he stared at the ceiling he heard a swishing noise at the end of the room that was different from the usual wind sound when walking down the high street.

Swish ... ... Swish... ..... Swish... ... . BANG!

Suddenly Steve was struck across the back as though he had been hit by a pillow when he was having pillow fights with his brother during his early childhood. He started sweating. It had started up again. He gripped the bed with both hands and prepared himself for another blow.

Thud! This time the bed shook and jostled from side to side. Natalie woke up and gave a shocked "Arrgghh!" Steve stayed quiet and did not say a word. The whole room settled down and both of them went back to sleep again. The silence had an eerie anger to it as though something was being prepared behind their backs. Their privacy and peace was interrupted at 3.12 am as their small double bed began to rock gently and slowly lengthways. It gradually gained momentum until it was crashing against the wall behind their headboard. Natalie suddenly woke up shouting "Slava bog! Slava bog!" shaking her husband in a frenzied temper. She looked at the bottom of her bed and saw a white flickering figure of a skinny teenage boy wearing a 1930's school uniform holding onto the metal railing. He was pushing and pulling on it with a hideous grin, showing a mouthful of dreadful teeth in desperate need of dental attention. His appearance was crystal clear and his eyes were full of mischievous hatred of a society that had treated him badly. Steve just sat up and looked in total despair as his wife screamed in Ukrainian. The figure's face lost its smile and suddenly, like a flash, he disappeared and the bed went back to being still again. Suddenly, Alex came into the room wondering what the noise was. His mother quickly grabbed his arm, feeling very embarrassed what sort of explanation she could give him, as she knew the real truth would have a devastating effect on his life as well as their own.

Chapter 7

"So what do we do?" asked Natalie as she and her husband seated themselves on a bench in Regents Park. Steve stayed silent as he just stared at the Post Office tower in the distance, chewing on his thumb nail. The two of them had decided to go out to London to discuss their home problems. Steve had kept quiet about what he had done during Natalie's absence in the Ukraine as he knew that she was easily upset.

"I think the best thing we should do at the moment is just play it cool. Another exorcism would just annoy these spirits all the more. There is no guarantee they will ever go. Perhaps we should just learn to live with it and in the end it might just leave on its own accord." Natalie just frowned as she was expecting her husband to come up with a better and more courageous answer. On the other hand it might be the best idea of all. The problem still remained that they still had to explain this to their son Alex. They knew that the spirits and entities, once ejected, could retaliate with a vengeance and even follow you to your next home.

"Look, Natalie, I want to sort this whole daft problem out from start to finish, I want to contact the local council and get the history on the land. I feel totally spellbound by this whole damn thing."

"Well you just make this good, Steve, if you don't, I'm sleeping in the car and I mean it," Natalie replied.

A scruffy unshaven man in his early thirties wearing

faded blue jeans and a grey Levi sweatshirt pulled up in a Singer Vogue down the side of Alexander Avenue. He was in the car alone and he had just finished listening to the last top ten hits on Radio Caroline. As he got out he carried a large plumber's tool bag and made his way up the short gravelled driveway to the large mechanic's garage that stood at the top of it. He stood to attention as he knocked on the rolling shutter.

Knock ... Tap, Tap, Tap ... Knock, knock

This was the secret code that was required to gain access to the premises where a very secret, grim, esoteric gathering took place twice a week. An older man opened a side door, ushered him inside without a word and walked across the workshop floor to a room at the back, which was used as the manager's office. The curtains were drawn and the electric light was switched on. Here, all four men and one woman in her late forties met to perform a satanic ritual. There, on the heavy oak table in a small caged pet carrier, was a black British short hair cat. It purred loudly and occasionally its eyes blinked. It was of skinny build and its collar and name tag had been removed. It was now 9.05 pm and all five of them stripped down to their underclothes and pulled out their totally black attire from carrier holdalls. They all helped each other pull on cloaks made of thick coarse wool that had resembled the druids that frequented Stonehenge. The group leader, an elderly man in his fifties, donned a cloak with mystical icons all over its front and back, resembling Jimmy Page's stage costume of the seventies.

"We shall begin now," he said in a quiet, mellow, dramatic voice as all five of them made their way, one behind the other, out of the office to the centre of the workshop floor. They all linked hands and shut their eyes for a few minutes. Nobody said a word. There was just silence. Suddenly the lead man broke the biting atmosphere with Gregorian chanting with a bass baritone voice while the other four replied with euphoric singing in tongues.

"Sheeeeervah!"... "Sheeeeeevah!"... "Heerhah!"...
"Heerhah!" … "Keerhah!"

They broke the circle and all of them, with stony expressions on their faces, stood to attention one more time with their hands by their sides. The twitching cat was pulled from its cage and forced to lie across a thin bench with its stomach pointing upwards. An old Nazi dress dagger was drawn from its scabbard, still with its original inscription visible on its flashing blade. It was handed with great care to the leader, who took it, clasping both hands around the black ivory handle. Holding it high above his head he held it for five endless seconds until, with the blink of an eye, the deadly instrument was plunged downwards into the defenceless animal's heart. There was an unforgettable long howl from the sad pathetic animal as the executioner's posture stayed like a statue, his face of grim satisfaction unchanged for some time, as the ground below lay smothered in blood. With the dagger laid next to the bench, the five men linked hands and chanted a verse for a full minute. The dead animal was wrapped in several large pages of the Observer news paper and was taken out of the back door by the least important member of the gang. A three feet deep hole was dug by the hedge at the bottom of the back yard as the corpse was carefully and silently placed at the bottom of it. The newspaper that it was wrapped in was by now saturated in dark red blood and bore the date at the top of its page. It was November 17 1968. As the man carried out this dishonorable gruesome task he was totally oblivious of a twitching Dralon curtain on the opposite side of the street. This demonic ritual had been carefully observed for the past four months and now the suspicious neighbours had made the brave decision to contact their local police station on the northern side of town. Their next meeting, the following Wednesday, was to be their last. A team of plain clothes police officers raided the premises just as their meeting was about to end and the entire gang was placed under arrest. So ended the tale of the infamous occult gang that was tried at County Hall Law Court in Kingston upon Thames in March 1969 and sent to prison for eighteen months. Their grisly practice would spiritually scar the ground for the innocent home that would be built on the same plot during the years that followed.

There was a turn of the key as Natalie arrived home from doing the daily shopping. As they only owned one car, Natalie had to carry the heavy carrier bags from the supermarket, thus causing her to have strained arms and shoulders.

"When the hell is my husband going to get me a bloody car?" she groaned to herself as she ran a hot bath to relieve her aching back. She was at home alone and was quite relieved to have her own space, listening to the radio for an hour while she relaxed in the steam filled bathroom. As Women's Hour started, she remembered that Suzie Quattro was to be interviewed by the programme's host, Andrea Kidd, who she had met by her husband's old school friend, David.

"Ah, Devil Gate Drive, December 1974," she recalled as her pop history was always very accurate from her teens. After a while of relaxing and washing, she dried herself very meticulously with a large white cotton beach towel and then gladly wrapped her slender, well-proportioned body in a pink bathrobe before lying on her bed and drifting off to sleep in a daytime slumber. Her mind glided peacefully over her social life of acquaintances from her adult education classes to her visits to the sauna at Fleet. As she slept with her body on one side she felt her left cheek being stroked by a very caring, caressing hand. Natalie didn't move or object as she pictured in her mind that it was her son or Steve that was doing so.

"What a charmer you are," she quietly said, thinking it was one of her family. The hand then continued to stroke and brush her long brunette hair for some time until she decided to open her eyes and greet this person. She turned her head and to her astonishment could see that she was still alone in the room.

"Steve, Steve!" she barked out as though she had been abandoned by her lover. There was no reply to her calling as she stood up and walked into the lounge, searching for the person that had woken her up. Every room was unoccupied.

"Come out, whoever you are!" she commanded in her Soviet voice. The whole home stayed silent. Then, after a long search, she lay on the sofa to let her mind recover from its confused state. Whatever showed interest in her could do so again. Suddenly Natalie felt an electric buzzing at her feet that worked along her legs like powerful electric voltage going past her at walking speed.

"Arrgghh!" she cried out as she was jolted sideways to the severe blow of strong energy with a burning sensation. As she glanced up she saw a glimpse of a short figure wearing an Edwardian style dress disappear through the adjoining wall at the far end of the dining room area. Natalie sat up on the sofa, recalling all that had happened with a shocked but not amused expression on her sharp eastern European face. She then heard a distinctive click as though some sort of force had left the room.

"Surely other people have had the same experiences as us," she whispered to herself. Her question would soon be answered in the fullness of time, as life's mystical timing of chance would soon reveal.

Chapter 8

All three of them sat around the breakfast table keenly devouring their fried eggs on toast, except Alex who had been addicted to Kellogg's Sugar Puffs from an early time since his arrival in England. Steve was busy reading all his daily mail, especially the letter from the Halifax Building Society.

"You know, Natalie, I think we were conned into the wrong mortgage. We needn't have got ourselves an endowment mortgage after all. I'm sure we could have got ourselves a repayment one."

"You didn't have to get this bloody home in the first place," Natalie replied in an annoyed tone.

"Well, I'm going to fix an appointment to get this garbage changed," he said with an authoritative tone to his voice.

Steve pushed open the highly polished door of the High Street branch and boldly strutted his way to the reception desk.

"I've come to see Jan Harper about changing my mortgage to a repayment one. My name is Steve Harrison from 3 Harley Meadows." The receptionist smiled and checked her appointment book.

"Ah yes, we have got you down, but Jan Harper is off sick today with that awful flu bug that's been going around, but don't worry, Sue Newell can fill in and help you with your new requirements. Please take a seat and she'll be with you in a minute."

Steve was not at all impressed, as his tough upbringing in

London had taught him to turn up for work if one was ill or not.

"Damn sickies," he mumbled to himself as his eyes drifted around the reception area. He caught sight of the usual bank advertising leaflets for loans, insurance and pensions.

"Loans, huh, I'm up to my bloody neck in bloody loans," he grumbled to himself.

A middle aged woman with a young toddler pushed her pin number in to the cash point machine a few metres away, the child thinking that her mother was going to buy her a new present and getting quite grizzly about her mother's reply.

"Hmmm, how much longer do I have to sit here?" groaned Steve. The queue at the reception counter grew longer then suddenly from the back office the door opened and a tall slim lady in her late twenties appeared, with blonde bobbed hair, wearing a dark blue skirt and white blouse.

"Mr Harrison," she called, looking in his direction .

"Yes, that's me," he replied in a tone that said, "I hope I've not come on a wasted journey."

The two of them sat down at a small table in the corner of the office and she broke the silence. "Harley Meadows, I used to live there at number five, just opposite where you live." Then her face changed to a confused frown.

"Have you noticed anything strange about where you live? Have you noticed that sometimes things move around by themselves?" Steve went very silent when he heard this and decided not to give anything away. Sue then stabbed at the heart of the beast.

"Have you seen a strange cloudy thing in your home yet?"

Steve started sweating and replied, "Well, I have heard of huge strange appearances but I can't make any sense of it." Sue replied, "It's all right, it doesn't matter, crazy weird place."

Fifty minutes later, Steve had finished his appointment and

had signed up with a new repayment mortgage, but through this appointment he had learnt that the previous owners had the same paranormal problem.

On his return to his home he was full of total bewilderment. He flicked on the electric kettle

and tossed all his new documents onto the double bed, before pacing the lounge and diner scratching the side of his face and rubbing his brow. "Why us? What the hell for? There has got to be an answer," he whispered to himself in a murmuring demand. The answer lay in front of him on the large glass. He went over to the sideboard and pulled out a large pad of paper and soon set to work by writing all the letters of the alphabet from A to Z with a thick black marker pen; all that was needed to make a homemade Ouija board was ready in ten minutes. Steve spread the cards all around the table, his heart beating faster as his forehead began to sweat.

"Now for the final touch," he said with triumph. He fetched a whisky glass from the kitchen and placed it in the middle of the table . By now his heart was pounding so heavily that warm sweat was seeping through his cotton shirt, as he placed his right finger on top of the glass and held it there for a full minute. The silence of the house made Steve all the more nervous in full anticipation as to what would happen in the next few minutes.

"Is there anybody there?" ... "Is there anybody there?" ... "If there is, please move the glass."

The glass remained still for thirty seconds until it slowly skated off to the letter J.

"My God, we're off!" The glass then glided slowly back to the centre and then to the letter O and then Y, C and E.

"Joyce," Steve thought in his mind.

Then he nervously cried out, " Do you have a message for me, Joyce?"

The glass then moved off to the "yes" card.

"What is your message?" he whispered in a very nervous tone.

"You are in very grave danger," the cards spelled out.

"What do you mean?"

"They seek revenge, yes you have made them very angry and they intend to get rid of you," the glass continued. This was enough for Steve and he pulled his finger off the glass, his heart pounding like a bass guitar. He knew who these upset people were, the spirits he had tried to exorcise three weeks before.

The following evening all three of them spent their time at Alex's football training. Natalie thought it would be good as she could meet all the other mums for a gossip and get to know

others for possible friendship. Steve was just glad to get out of the house to have a good shout and de-stress himself of all the aggravation he had been under.

"That Monica was very nice to chat to, she's not a snob of any kind," said Natalie as she pulled on her seat belt.

"Yeah," said Steve in a very weary drawl, his mind on what had happened the previous afternoon. "Look, I think we should get off home, Alex wants a bath and so do I. I feel myself stinking."

As the two of them lay in bed, Steve just lay there with his hands behind his head while his wife completed her training application for a teacher's post that she has been advised to do by a colleague from Marks and Spencer.

"They are crying out for Maths teachers in England and the pay is pretty good," sighed Natalie.

"The only snag is how good are you with kids?" added Steve. He was very glad to hear this news as the family needed a good second income. He was trying to look on the positive side. With the bedside digital clock showing 11.35 pm, Natalie turned out the light and they both settled down in bed together for a full seven hours and some sweet talk.

It was 2.40 am in the morning and Steve was having a touch of cramp in his left leg. He woke up quite quickly and turned over to get the attention of his wife.

"What's Natalie doing out of bed?" he thought as he rolled over and looked to his right. In the darkness of the room he saw a solid black figure of an old woman sitting upright on the side of the bed. The figure looked very sad and still and was in need of attention. As Steve rolled over to do so he saw to his total astonishment that Natalie was asleep beside him.

"Who is this third person in our bedroom?"

He gripped the bed and lay still, observing the figure that sat there about four feet away; all that could be seen was its back and head, all very clearly. During the next twenty minutes, very gradually, the woman in black disappeared. Steve took in all that he saw, not amused and also very shocked, then like all the previous times before he had to try and get back to sleep and do a day's work the following day.

"I've put plenty of mustard in your ham sandwiches."

"Ta, love," whispered Steve as they said goodbye to each other on the doorstep. Ten minutes later he was speeding on the slip road which took him onto the M3 motorway as he remained deadpan and silent as the thoughts of the previous night flashed through his mind. Smooth radio started to play persistent second rate chart songs. "Oh, push off," growled Steve in a very irritated voice and then stabbed at the off button on the dashboard stereo. The car went silent as the drone of the motorway was all that could be heard. He got as far as Lightwater when a firm dominant grip of the steering wheel began to steer it in a vice-like grip towards the central reservation.

"Damn! … Hell! ... Damn! What the bloody hell's going on, man?" Steve yelped as the car careered from the middle lane into the fast lane, hot and cold sweat running from his forehead and body.

"God help me!" He clasped the wheel and with all his might pulled the car back into the middle lane as he almost hit a Volkswagen Passat coming up from behind. He knew this was some supernatural occurrence and no mechanical fault of the car, as all the tell-tale signs were there as some body or force was behind the wheel trying to cause a crash. Steve's whole back turned to pins and needles as the vehicle accelerated from 75 to 98 mph by itself with a mystery foot on the gas pedal. Again the steering wheel span from right to left as Steve fought frantically to keep control, gritting his teeth and bawling, "No you don't, you son of a bitch!" He pulled the wheel back again as it careered towards the central reservation, his whole suit drenched with sweat. By the time he reached Staines he had regained control of the car and was overcome with tearful emotion. He pulled over at the slip road which led the way to the A30, tears of despair pouring down his cheeks.

"Oh hell, oh bloody hell!" The car quickly restored itself to normal as Steve literally prayed to God that this normality would hold out until he got to Hatton Cross underground station. As the driver's seat soaked up all the perspiration from his traumatic ordeal, the road sign for central London came in sight, insinuating that he had won the first round to his chilling, defying passenger.

"Hey man, you look as though you've seen a ghost," cackled the Jamaican sounding car park attendant as he gave a fixed penalty ticket to an old Ford Mondeo. Steve looked back at him and replied, "Never a true word said in jest," and the coloured man squealed/ shouted? with laughter as most West Indians do. He then strolled back to his small pokey portacabin, took off his gloves and started reading his daily copy of the *Sun* newspaper. After collecting his pay and display sticker from the far end machine, Steve quickly strutted off to the tube station to catch the Piccadilly line to take him to the docklands in East London for an operations meeting, while his car stayed put, the handbrake full on and every window wound up. The only sounds that could be heard were of jet aircraft going overhead and noisy cars driving past. The car park attendant finished off his chicken tikka sandwich and Quavers and began his boring monotonous stroll around the compound, checking every windscreen and window for non-payment.

With the sound of Bob Marley still echoing in his head he came to Steve's car.

"Huh, hey what?!"

He stopped dead in his tracks as he looked frozen, bolt upright, glaring, staring and totally transfixed, at the driver's seat. There sat a very tall gangly man wearing an old fashioned prison uniform, with dark blonde greasy hair and his arms folded in a most uninviting manner, while his head was in a forward, bowed position.

"Hey! Is this another car thief or what, man?" he objected in his thick Jamaican drawl. He leant down and tapped on the driver's window to disturb the driver from what he intended on doing . At first the figure did not stir, then the man tapped again and the figure began to lift his head slowly in a stiff robotic manner, as though one could call it unnatural. He turned his head slowly to the attendant and then looked at him for about three seconds. His face looked ashen and had a wooden expression to it, then slowly his whole face transformed into a laughing, snarling appearance.

His eyes were a dark yellow colour, like organ stops, his teeth khaki and unkempt as though they were victims of sheer neglect. Choking on his breath, the attendant recoiled backwards, his eyes totally transfixed and paralyzed on what he had just seen. Taking three steps backwards in a slow

45

manner he returned to his kiosk, expecting refuge and protection there, his whole body convulsing with shock. An hour went by and he finally plucked up the courage to do his round at the car park again. After issuing two fixed penalty notices he approached the right final flank of cars, where Steve's Volvo was parked.

"Huh, son of a bitch," the attendant whispered in total fear and bother as there at the end of the compound stood the man that had been sitting at the wheel, leaning against the car with his arms crossed with a piercing stare and an almost snarling, schizophrenic smile. The attendant had to walk past him to finish his round and with nimble steps, the man's head turned to keep his eyes on him without a blink. The man stayed stationary for the rest of his shift until Steve returned. The coloured attendant looked at Steve with tremendous greeting and he just replied, "Alright mate," in response to this.

"Hey, man, you certainly have some weird dudes for friends."

"Sorry, mate, I'm not with you," Steve replied.

"That big ugly guy that sat in your car all morning and then leaned and glared at me since 1.30 this afternoon. Over six foot, he was."

Steve looked back at him, totally lost and confused. The memories of the morning were still with him and he shyly opened the door, got in and started the engine. Suddenly he stopped. The ash tray had been fully pulled out and the whole car stank of stale cigarette smoke and a sweaty body smell. He checked all around him and it seemed that nothing else had been tampered with. In response to this rank smell, he flicked his door switch to wind down the window and then he drove off. By now it was starting to get dark and he turned on the heater to get rid of the biting chill that had taken root in the car. The traffic news seemed very good, which was most unusual for that time in the evening. As he drove home with the window down, the dirty odour did not clear with the hypnotic street lights on the M3 flashing through his car with monotonous regularity. By now the palms of his hands had begun to sweat on the warm steering wheel, as the thoughts of what had happened that morning began to repeat in his mind, with hot and cold flushes running up and down his back and legs. As he checked his driver's mirror he was in for an even more shocking experience. A tall figured body began to appear in the centre of the rear passenger seat. It just stayed there until Steve drove as far as Bagshot, while the terrible smell in the car grew stronger. It was transparent black with a long slender face and hollow temples. The figure did not move, in fact it disappeared and so did the grotty smell. Steve stayed stiff, cool and disciplined all the time until he reached his drive way outside their bungalow. His face was totally pale and drawn, and once he had unfastened his seat belt, he put his forehead on the rim of the steering wheel and wept with despair.

Chapter 9

Ten months had gone by since their arrival at Harley Meadows and it had been a mixture

of euphoria and bewilderment. The Harrison family had made contact with the Russian Orthodox church in London W4 through Natalie, as she was advised not to seek help from any other Christian denomination regarding the issues with their home.

As both of them climbed out of the Piccadilly line underground train to attend the ten o'clock morning service, they felt a new assurance could be a new chance to break the grip that was holding their home in an occultic fist.

"These people at the end of the road are Ukrainian. They don't look English," proclaimed Natalie in a voice with a knowing eye.

"Well, in that case we know we've come to the right place," said Steve, as he was certainly in no mood to go trekking around west London in search of any other church. As they neared the front car park on that warm sunny Sunday morning, they could hear hymn singing getting louder and louder from a well sung Russian choir. The great architecture at the front was all inspiring with its great stained glass windows displaying its orthodox icons in the sunlight.

"Do you know which one is Father Gapon out of all those bods in black?" whispered Steve as they all slowly made their way through the very dark entrance to the overcrowded altar at the front.

"He's the man standing second from the left holding the incense and heavy crucifix." Natalie had spoken to him on the telephone and had made the appointment to speak to him at the end of the service. Steve grew restless as the service seemed to go on forever, while an old woman with old fitting caps and crowns on her teeth pulled at his sleeve for a donation to their end of service coffee meeting. "Oh, OK, here you are," he reluctantly groaned as he slipped from his jacket pocket an extra large Snickers bar he was looking forward to afterwards.

"Do we have to stay here any longer?" he moaned.

His wife snapped back, "Just be patient," as the sound of Gregorian chanting echoed all around them. An orthodox priest swinging his bells and smells added a putrid odour wherever he went as an old woman was laid out in her coffin to the far right of the church.

"Makes you glad to be alive, doesn't it ?"

"Shhhh," sounded an old woman in front of him.

As Natalie stepped forward to take her communion she gave a brief message to the priest who slightly nodded and hinted to him after. They knew that he was the only man who could offer advice as he had carried out exorcisms in Siberia years before his arrival in England. Parents had bought children and other family members to him that had been possessed by spirits where spiritualism was rife. Many of these victims were forced to the ground howling and snarling like dogs until the spirit was cast out.

An hour later in the minister's vestry all three of them met and Natalie explained the full scenario about their home.

"They have dug up the sewers and all hell has broken loose. All I can do is give you an explanation and come over to your home and try and cure it. There is no guarantee I can get rid of it all." Steve explained about all the different types of ghost they had had. Father Gapon replied in a rather matter or fact tone.

"You and your family could become possessed by two different types of ghost. First there are the souls of deported people. These ghosts have the personality of the deceased and the free will to decide what to do after death of their physical body, so far as they are aware that they are dead. Many of these ghosts have overseen their death and try to live as though they have not died. The other category are shows of departed people, such as an astral body left behind on the journey to higher realms. Both kinds of ghost affect people and possess them."

Steve tried to react as though he knew what he meant by this but he decided not to show his ignorance.

"Ghosts can possess people for many reasons. The most common case occurs because the ghost needs a living person's energy in order to survive. Other reasons include their attachment to normal human life and because they don't want to leave their family and friends. I know I can talk to the ghost and get to know where it originated from and where it lived and died. Exorcising ghosts is very difficult work and rather dangerous, and it's possible that every room may need exorcising rituals every day for up to three months . However, my method is very safe and successful. Sometimes one or more ghosts can possess an entire house, thus called a haunting, but it is difficult to exorcise haunted places. The exorcist must contact each ghost and explain the situation and fully convince it to go to the other side in the so called "Heaven to God." But many of them fear they will go to purgatory or hell and so they will resist leaving.

Hell can't be accepted by certain ghosts, especially if they have died under tragic or traumatic circumstances. If its alright with you both I would like to come to your home Thursday week at 11 am because this is the time that I feel that I can get to meet the spirits that I feel are the matters in question."

Steve and Natalie automatically accepted Gapon's offer

without any further ado and, as they gave their address, they left by the back door with hardly a word to say.

"So what do we do then?" whispered Natalie. " We've got no option but to go for it, for hell or high water," with a 'got no other option in the world' tone.

"We can't live like this and we can't suffer any more so we've got to come out fighting. If the bloody thing wants to retaliate then I'm waiting for it," growled Steve.

"Well, if that's the case then I'm right behind you. He who dares wins. Is that what Trotter said?" drawled Natalie.

"Yes," groaned Steve. "Right, then that's settled then."

The two of them got up out of their plastic seats, shoveled their tray of rubbish into the McDonalds litter bin and walked out of the double swing doors to the Knightsbridge Central line tube station.

During the past few nights they had had a few strange occurrences. A sparkling shadow drifted into the room giving off a pulsating, juddering sensation, while it came to a stop over Steve and then drifted around the bed and disappeared though the wall behind their headboard. He decided to tell his wife about this the morning they set off to see Father Gapon. Natalie had felt something touch her shoulder, which felt like a push from a very cold hand. She thought it was Alex and one of his jokes, but when she turned around there was nobody there. All this had become all too familiar and they were getting very tired of it. What started out as a thrilling experience had become a very wearing strain. All of them battled on for another eleven days until their one and only saving grace, Father Gapon, would arrive.

It was late Thursday morning and Gapon finally arrived half an hour late due to last minute enquiries at his church. As he was finally greeted at the front door, his thick dark suit and black brogue shoes certainly convinced the Harrison family that he meant business with what had been discussed the previous week. In his small tatty brown suit case was a golden cassock, heavily decorated with silver and gold braid with many icons and crucifixes. Accompanying this was a large bottle of holy water and garlic. As he started unpacking everything on the dining room table he hardly said a thing. In fact, he stayed very silent and kept his eyes on his personal effects. When Natalie asked him if he wanted any tea or coffee he tersely said, "No, no, NO!" His face was stiff and iron looking as though he was going to do business with a formidable opponent. Both Steve and Natalie gave a detailed rundown on what had happened since they last met, but Gapon did not give any emotional reaction at all as he slipped off his heavy jacket and handed it to Natalie whilst holding his breath and pulling on his heavily decorated cassock.

"Open all the windows," he snapped in a rather irate tone and immediately reached for his bottle of holy water, unscrewing the plastic cap and tossing great handfuls in all directions regardless of electrical appliances. He then lifted up his large bronze crucifix at face level and broke the silence by speaking and chanting in tongues with a powerful tenor voice for three minutes.

A powerful silence gripped the room while Gapon stood there bolt upright, his eyes getting wider and wider until he ordered in a thick Russian accent, "What do you want with this home?" "What do you want with this family?"

An angry silence was thrown back in Father Gapon's face as his head tilted back as though a revolting stench had been placed under his nose.

"No, in the blood of Jesus and holy God, this is forbidden!"

His whole body convulsed as he pushed his way further until he came to a dead end stop, standing still as though he was rooted to the ground. Thrusting out his crucifix he started chanting Russian, which got louder and louder as he pushed his way forward. Suddenly, from the corner of the living room, came a totally un-describable feminine scream like a witch being burned at the stake. Nobody could see it but the energy of massive electricity could be clearly felt.

"Nooooooooo! Arrrgggghhhhh! Arrrgggghhhhhh!"

Steve and Natalie recoiled backwards to the other end of the room as they had suddenly noticed a shadow of a small scrawny figure couched by the sideboard with very long unkempt hair. Gapon did not relent to any mercy as he kept the crucifix trained on this pathetic figure, his voice persistently and loudly pelting the atmosphere with Russian Gregorian chanting commanding the entity to be banished and taken to a place of unrelenting exile. Fifteen minutes later, with the priest on his knees and giving the final barrage of spiritual repulsion, the screaming and howling finally stopped.

But for Father Gapon, his job was far from finished. He climbed to his feet and was hungry for more, as he started again repeating what he had done twenty minutes before. With his heavy bronze cross held out in sheer defiance, he took tentative steps to Alex's bedroom. As he stood in front of the door he made the sign of the cross as they do in the orthodox church and then opened the door slowly as if he was to expect an ambush. A strange sound occurred as though a vacuum seal had been broken and then a gruff coughing noise came from the chair in the far corner. *Clunk.* The crucifix was knocked from his hand as he began to interrogate the entity as to why he had defied the previous exorcism.

"This is my home and I was called here against my wishes many years before. I will not be pushed around like this. I was killed by an electric shock when I was forty one. I want justice for my death and to who pushed me onto the railway line. I want to be left alone in peace."

Without his crucifix Father Gapon could not sustain the energy that was needed to remove the entity and all he could do was to talk to the spirit and explain the reasons for his visit.

The spirit was a demonic, angry individual who had been an alcoholic in a previous life and his noisy, aggressive manner had refused to leave him, being so resentful of all the opposition he had received since his death.

"I have nothing against the woman or the boy, but I want that clever arse bastard sorted out!"

"Do you mean Steve Harrison?"

"Yes, of course, that's the bloke. You can flaming well tell him that I've got it in for him!"

Gapon abruptly replied, "Steve hasn't anything against you, he just wants his family cared for."

"But who cares for me?" the spirit replied.

"If you want to escape from this dimension that you have been called to then look to the light.

There you can pass over to the spirit world and you'll be free from the chains that enslaved you in this life. You must take my advice or I shall return with the power and authority to evict you from this place that only has yourself imprisoned and others as well. I shall go now but I must warn you that I have the power to return and fight."

"You cant keep me out of my home to satisfy your ego. I have the right to a settled home and it's in your interest to just leave me be!"

"I can't do that. Your interests are malignant and I can't allow you to share this home with this innocent family. I must still ask you to leave." There was a stiff hostile silence as Gapon reached slowly across the room and opened the window to the fully opened position.

"I'm telling you to go now. Go now!"

There was an angry silence and a black angry shadow got up from the chair and drifted towards the window. Five seconds later there was a distinctive click and Gapon's ears popped before he crept forward and shut the window. He scratched the back of his head and sighed, "Let's hope he doesn't return." After retrieving his cross and shutting the door behind him, he turned his attention to the larger bedroom at the end of the hall, with his chin up high and a deathly cold breeze brushing his face. On the bed sat black shadowy figures of a young boy and older man in his fifties. Gapon took a much softer approach to the boy as he could see that he was in a difficult position.

"I'm being bullied and held by this cruel man that has held this home in an iron fist. I have to be his servant or I am threatened with purgatory." This was very difficult as Father Gapon had to break the spiritual hold that the man had on the home before the young boy could be released.

The old man growled in a threatening voice, "The more you try it with me, the more the boy gets it. You priests think you can get rid of me, well, you can just go to hell and rot."

"Who are you? What's your name?" shouted Gapon.

"So why should I tell you? You have no business here. You raise your cross to us and the boy can sod off and come back at a later time. He's mine. Is that clear?"

"There is no way anyone can reason with you, is there?" replied Gapon in a very strong sarcastic tone.

"I know how you priests work. One more move and I'll take it out on the lad."

The shrewd priest retreated backwards to the door, keeping his eyes fixed on the two figures as he did so.

Steve and Natalie were waiting nervously in the lounge for the uncertain news from Gapon's mission around their home. Eventually he looked at them both face to face with a blank enigmatic expression as though he was doubtful on the conclusion he had met. "I have some very complicated news to explain. It seems that you have two spirits that have refused to leave. They see you, Steve, as the person that wants to throw down the gauntlet and they are prepared to fight you for the possession of this home. At this moment in time I can't shift them until I can find more information to break their hold on this place. For the time being I suggest you sleep in the lounge at night to avoid further bloodshed."

Chapter 10

Alex sat in a slouched position on the sofa restlessly switching television channels on cable TV. He sighed and whinged to himself as all his other school friends were out amusing themselves doing other things . In other words he was " blown out" by his friends and Cartoon Network had very little to offer in compensation for his lack of company. He got up and wandered into the kitchen where his mother was busy doing the washing. With a childish whining voice he moaned to his mother, "Mum, I don't like it here. I haven't any real friends and nobody wants to talk to me."

It was the typical line that we all, at some stage in our lives, were guilty of giving our parents. Natalie was in a filthy terrible mood and very disappointed with her lot as she snapped and screamed back.

"Alex, I have no friends either. I hate my life here and I'm bloody not happy, so that bloody makes two of us. I have enough problems without listening to your moaning. I can't make friends for you so you'll just have to do something about it for yourself!"

Alex began to cry, and the more he cried the more his mother shouted at him. Natalie turned off the television and in her anger and frustration threw the remote control across the lounge, which landed by the curtains with a cracking sound. What followed next was a very nasty slanging match in Ukrainian as both mother and son released their emotions on each other and Alex got himself in more of a state with his attitude. He then stormed into his bedroom, threw himself on the bed and cried his eyes out with his head buried in the pillow.

After about fifteen minutes Alex heard a voice calling to him outside his bedroom window.

"Whatchya! Whatchya doin'?" Alex looked up .

There outside was a young boy of about twelve wearing new jeans and a light green T shirt. He looked through the window at Alex and said, "What ya crying for?"

"Oh, nothing," replied Alex in a sudden change of mood, almost glad that somebody had shown some interest in him.

"D'ya like football?"

"Sure I do," replied Alex and before he knew what had happened he grabbed his ball from the wardrobe, climbed out of the window and started talking to the boy.

"I'm James and I've just moved into the next street in Edward Avenue."

"I'm Alex and I come from the Ukraine."

The two of them accepted each other immediately and then headed over the back of the estate where there was an area of disused scrub land surrounded by thick bushes and trees.

"I know, let's set up two goals and see who can score the most!"

After an hour the boys chatted persistently about their hobbies, football and games being the most popular, and it was quite clear that the two had found each other.

"That big tree over there, I bet you can't climb it!"

"I bet you I can!" shouted Alex. The two found foot holes in the trunk and climbed up to the fifth row of branches and they both sat on the thickest one.

"I come from Macclesfield up north near Manchester," said James. "Me dad works for BP at Sunbury, examining rocks for oil," in a broad Cheshire accent.

"My stepdad's a sales rep for an air cargo company at the

airport," sighed Alex, as if he wanted to give Steve a better title he could be really proud of. The two boys had only been together three hours and it soon became apparent that they had become the very best of friends.

"Who do you support?" enquired James.

"West Ham United," replied Alex.

"Ah, they're the real gear," replied James. "That Trevor Brooking's a real dream weaver," he added.

Alex was very confused as he didn't know of any player by the name of Trevor Brooking in the West Ham squad. He didn't want to put James down as he certainly knew his stuff about football teams.

"Look, I think I've got to go now, my mum's bound to be getting lunch up soon at one o'clock."

James looked very sad and down-hearted and pleaded that he wanted to meet up with Alex that afternoon.

"Sure I will," he replied and the two of them parted company with gleeful faces that fun and friendship had come into their lives.

"Ah, Alex, I was about to call you. Where have you been?" asked his mother as she briskly stirred a saucepan of spaghetti Bolognese on a well lit gas hob.

"Guess what, mum, I've found a new friend and we've had such a great time!"

"Really, my boy, and next time you shoot off like this would you mind telling where you've gone?" replied his mother in a rather sarcastic tone.

"But we played football over the back and explored the ditch and climbed the old oak tree. Can I invite him round for tea?"

"What?" she replied. "Well, just get to know the boy a bit longer and find out if he's a real friend and not a hooligan."

As soon as Alex finished his lunch, he squeezed on his smelly trainers and fled outside again and sure enough, a few doors down, sitting on the wall outside number seven was James. The two boys' faces lit up and off they both ran to the recreation ground at Dingle Road.

"I know, let's play with these stones, skimming across them across the canal, and see who can hit the mooring post on the other side. Do you see it?"

"Yahoo!" cried Alex as on the fifth occasion he hit it with a great cracking sound. "Bulls-eye!" shouted James as the stone skimmed with great accuracy and hit it head on. After forty minutes the two of them walked to the top of the grass verge and lay down together, propping themselves up with their forearms and talking about their lives and parents.

"Me dad's a great bloke but he's always coming home late. Ya know, he always spends two hours in the pub each night and comes home an hour before I go t'bed," said James.

Alex felt that he could really talk to James as he was looking for a friend he could really pour out his heart to. "My mum's Ukrainian from the old Soviet Union times, they're really strict and they are always shouting at me and telling me off," moaned Alex.

"You should get out more, old son, and ya know I'm always about in the evening so we can always meet up and 'ave some fun, ya know like."

"Oh great, really, I'd love to," exclaimed Alex. "If you want to you can round to my home for tea and play on the computer, my mum won't mind!"

James suddenly went all quiet and shy. "Well, I can't say yes and I can't say no, ya see I've got to be home and help me ma in the kitchen and do me 'omework." Alex tried to be tactful and not to push it.

"When shall we meet next?"

"Ya what?" said James.

"I mean shall I see you Monday," said Alex.

"Yeah, that'll be great," said James. "I'll be waiting for ya by those trees at the back where we played soccer"

"Ace," replied Alex . The two boys reluctantly parted as Alex headed back to his bungalow and James headed back to Edward Avenue in the next street.

"Haven't seen you all afternoon," said Steve in a voice that indicated he was relieved to see his young boy back all safe and sound. "Yeah, had a really great time," replied Alex as he took off his shoes in the hallway to his mother's orders. "Spent all afternoon playing with a great new mate at the rec called Jim or James, but he comes from up north near Manchester. He really knows all about football and all the players from the world cup Mexico. Steve, can he come round for tea and play just like it was before I came to England? He's a real good mate and we both love football."

"Yeah, OK, but check that it's all OK with your mother. She's just moaned all day about the state of this place and I've just had a right skinful of her recently."

Alex gleefully switched his X-Box on and began to play his DVD video game. His mind began to ponder on how he would amuse and entertain James when he would come over and between the two of them would bond a really great comradeship. There would be no more boring weekends being bossed about by his mother and being moaned at by Steve.

"Hooray!" went his heart, feeling euphoria that he had found a road out of the rut that he was in.

"Mum, can I invite James to tea and play, Steve says it's all OK?"

"Oh .... OK then but as long as there is no horseplay.".

"Yes!" and he ran around the lounge practicing his new football moves.

The next afternoon Alex prepared his invitation. Instead of a grateful acceptance from James, he was given a very sullen and regretful refusal. "Can't," whined James . "What! Why not?" demanded Alex.

"Got to be at home, me mum's really strict and she says that I've got to be home by eight o'clock."

"Well, that's OK, my dad can drive us home to your house." There was a cold silence for a few minutes then James's face lifted. "OK then, ta, next Thursday then alright?"

"Yes, that's great," said Alex in a hasty but happy voice. Alex didn't care what night it was just as long as he could have a good mate round for the evening. The two of them headed off to the rec to play on the rope that was suspended over the canal and do Tarzan impressions.

"AArrgghh … AArrgghh," in flat yodeling tones. The two boys just laughed and laughed until the muscles in their faces throbbed.

Creeeaaak! … Snap! … Splash! The rope snapped and James fell head first into the water. As he surfaced a few seconds later he was all covered in mud and moaned, "Aw, bloody 'eck," as he crawled on to the bank as his friend pulled him out with an amused but also not amused expression on his face. "You had better go home and get changed quick," said Alex, "otherwise you'll get pneumonia."

James seemed to react as though he was immune from all illnesses and they slowly wandered off down the A331 to their homes. Suddenly there was a roar of thunder which gave the introduction to a torrential downpour and after five minutes of running through the rain, a middle aged man wearing faded jeans and donkey jacket driving an old Ford transit van signaled to the kerb and pulled over to offer them a lift home.

"Oh great, Alex, let's go!" screamed James as they ran to the rusty vehicle and pulled back the passenger door.

"Where are you going to, boys?" said the man in a most obliging voice. As he looked across to his passenger side he smiled at Alex but when he looked at James his expression soon changed to a worried grimace.

"Can you take us to Edward Avenue, it's just off Frimley Park Hospital?" said Alex as they both

clambered in to the van and pulled on their safety belts. "Right, well, I can drop you off at the big roundabout as I'm just passing through." The two boys just looked at each other blankly as they had to trust the driver. About ten minutes after they got into the cab, the driver strangely started to get very nervous to a state of absolute panic. Finally they approached Edward Avenue, the van coming to an unexplainable stop as though some strange force or power had come over the engine or motion of the vehicle. Everyone in the cab stayed totally silent as though there was one minute's silence on Remembrance Day. Nobody even moved. Then James snatched the driver's spare work coat that was tucked down the side of the passenger seat, pulled back the door and ran off in the direction of his home address. A few seconds later, the remaining two of them suddenly snapped out of their dozy trance that had come over them and then pulled away from the kerb until Alex told the driver to drop him off at the end of Frimley Road.

"My God, you are absolutely soaked through!" screamed Natalie as Alex timidly opened the back door to the kitchen and tried to pull off his soaking trainers. "We both got a lift from this bloke and James says he can come over next Thursday about four o'clock," said Alex, as though he was trying to change the subject to a more positive one.

Later that evening, when Alex had had a hot bath supervised by his mother, he told Steve how keen he was to have James over for the evening the following Thursday . "Well, just as long as he hasn't been crowd diving in the local canal, he's more than welcome."

"Alex, I've just received your school report in the post this morning and I'm not happy. Your maths have slipped and if you don't pull your socks up you're going to be put down a group. When you come home from school on Monday you're not going out until your maths are up to standard again. You've been sent an exercise book that must be completed in time for your exam in ten days . I'll let James come over next Thursday but I insist that you spend the evening doing your maths revision. I' m not going to have you drop down a class." Alex knew that his mother was serious and didn't argue and he certainly didn't want to be associated with a class of dummies. He was better than that!

Brrriiinnnggg! The school bell sent shockwaves through the entire school as hundreds of scruffy kids with their shirt tails hanging out grabbed their shoulder bags and ran for the nearest exit. Alex had finished his art class and felt in jubilant mood and, after unlocking his mountain bike, made off at high speed to prepare all his football attire and amusements for his long awaited guest. Every minute he checked his watch to see how much longer he would have to wait for James to ring the doorbell to his bungalow. His hands began to sweat and his neck began to tingle as four o'clock came and went and there was no sign of his guest. It was now half past four and still no sound came from the door step of his home.

"Are you sure your friend has got his dates right, Alex?" enquired Natalie in a huffy, put out voice as she laid the table for their evening meal.

"Yes I am, mum. I just don't know why he hasn't come!"

"Do you know where he lives?" asked his mother, seeing that her son was getting very nervous and upset.

"Yes, its 47 Edward Avenue."

"Well, maybe you should go and knock on his door and go and find out what the problem is."

Alex's heart sank as he feared that his much looked forward to evening was about to go pear shaped, and with a totally gutted feeling pulled on his coat to walk to James's house. He turned the corner into Edward Avenue and reached the garden gate to number forty seven. It was a very old house with a grim green and white front door with an old concrete pathway leading to it. He knocked very hesitantly on the door using the chrome knocker that was high up near to the dull window that was at the top. Some time went by until an elderly man answered the door with a cut chin and several teeth missing down one side of his mouth.

"Hello, good afternoon. Can I speak to James, please?" The man gave a very strange look and replied in a gruff voice, "There's no one of that name lives here, have you tried next door?"

"No," replied Alex.

"Then you should give them a try. I've lived here for twenty one years and I've never heard of a lad called James." Alex was totally confused. Maybe he had got his figures wrong as he had done before. So back he ran to the end of the path way to try the house next door. Again he banged on the door and this time he got a quicker response, this time an old lady in her sixties, much surprised to see a young boy standing on her doorstep.

"Does James Patterson live here?"

The woman pulled a very enigmatic face and after several moments replied, "Well, I don't know how to answer that." Suddenly her face flickered and popped.

"No he doesn't, but oddly enough, the only James Patterson that I know, or knew, was the little boy that lived next door about twenty years ago. The Patterson family lived here for a couple of years until their young lad was knocked down and killed just along this road here, back in 1973 it must be. I remember he ran into the road after his football and an Austin Cambridge didn't stop in time. Oh, very sad. The family moved down here from up north, smashing family."

Alex recoiled backwards, absolutely speechless with what he had heard.

"But where is James now?" he asked the woman. "Oh, he was buried at St Michael's cemetery up at the top of the hill on the A30. I can take you there to see it if you want."

Alex stood there on the doorstep and couldn't accept all that he had heard in a very short space of time.

The lady said, "Look, love, let's take a walk, it's only ten minutes' walk away," and without any further ado she had pulled on her rain mac and flat soled shoes and off they went, both of them, to see the grave where James was buried. Alex explained to the lady, Audrey, that he had played with the young boy for the past two weeks. After a long walk and many shared memories, the two of them eventually reached the cemetery gates of rusty plain iron.

"Here, it's at the top just on the right of the pathway," said Audrey, almost out of breath and almost panting on her slightly asthmatic chest.

Alex suddenly stopped dead in his tracks, not because of the small gravestone that stood in front of him, but because there, hanging on the marble cross, was the van driver's grubby coat that James had taken that afternoon they were given a lift in the rain.

"My God! ... I just don't believe it!" exclaimed Alex in a slow drawl. As he stood there he read the gravestone inscription. "In Fond Remembrance of our Dear Son James Robert Patterson

Born 6 May 1961. Died 13 July 1973."

"There, look ! That's his headstone. I was at his funeral along with many others. His parents needed all the support they could get."

Alex momentarily stared at the grave with the soft blowing breeze whispering through his fine fair hair. Then slowly he stepped forward, collected the coat from the cross, folded it up and held it tight against his chest.

"If you want to stay longer then perhaps you should think

about getting yourself back home, young man," the woman advised in a firm voice.

As the two of them departed at the cemetery gates, Alex's walking pace increased to a slow trot as he headed back home, his face totally stone-like, trying to hold back the impossible explanation he had to tell his mother.

"I know what you mean, Steve, but this is beyond belief. If we were to stay any longer I see the whole picture turning from bad to worse. Whatever possesses this place has certainly got it in for us," whinged Natalie in an uncompromising tone. "That incident three months ago almost got you killed and I don't want you to go through that hell again."

"OK, OK, dear, but I think we should let sleeping dogs lie and hope that that the whole thing just settles down. If we get any more priests in or exorcism experts then we could just stir things up all the more."

With a heavy sigh the two of them carried their dirty crocks into the kitchen and made their way to the bedroom.

Chapter 11

"I'm just off to Ben's house to see the SKY sport!"

"OK, Alex," replied Steve in a relieved voice, as this meant that he could have some peace on Saturday morning. At about 10.30 he got out of bed and stepped into the shower, quickly adjusting the dials until he got a hot spray obtained by his fickle fingers. The noise of this ritual blocked out his hearing ability to what was going around him and with a palm full of shampoo he quickly created a full head of foam.

"Arrgghh, bloody hell!" he screamed as it all ran into his eyes. At that moment he thought he saw a shadow of a figure through the shower curtain and, wiping away the soap from his face, opened up the conversation.

"Ah, Natalie, what's happened, I wasn't expecting you home until two o'clock." There was no answer to his enquiring voice but Steve remained silent, thinking that his wife was in one of her grumpy staid moods that was typical of her personality.

"Bloody hell, Natalie, have you got that bloody door open again?" moaned Steve as a frosty wall of coldness glided past his soapy naked body. There was still no answer as he continued to cleanse his armpits and chest with the Radox shower gel that was unused since Christmas.

"Well, you can at least give me an answer, you grumpy cow," he uttered as the feminine shadowy figure on the other side of the shower curtain turned around and silently left the room without making any noise with the door.

Half an hour later, the tall Londoner had revived himself of all his ablutions and with steam as thick as a Turkish bath he stepped out onto the soft fluffy bath mat and grabbed a large warm bath towel from the airing cupboard. With his eyes gazing around he saw a message written in old copper plate writing on the steamed up bathroom mirror, "You will join us."

"What the hell's all this?" he whispered in a very melodramatic tone. With the towel around his waist and looking like Mahatma Gandhi, he stepped out of the bathroom.

"Natalie, what' s the big idea, love?" The whole bungalow remained silent, there was absolutely no reply. He walked into the lounge and all the bedrooms calling her name.

"Natalie … Natalie!" Still no reply. He stood in the hallway, his posture stiff and his face pale as a sheet.

"Oh no, bloody hell, not again!" The message in his mind echoed over and over again,

"You will join us, you will join us, you will join us."

"What do they mean? Is this a club?"

"No! They want to kill me!" A bolt of shivering went down his legs, the motive giving him a wave of profound shock before strutting back into the bathroom and frantically wiping out the slogan on the mirror with the side of his fist.

"Calm down, Steve my boy, calm down, nothing's going to harm you, pull yourself together, mate." He decided to keep this whole incident to himself as his family would explode into a session of panic.

That following Monday afternoon, Alex was finishing his English essay at school. With the last ten minutes dragging as he tentatively checked his watch, Oliver, his new friend who sat in front of him, turned around and whispered, "D'ya wanna go to Virgin after school?" He thought about the proposal for a few seconds and then gave the sign of, "OK, let's do it." With a quirky grin, Oliver turned around and finished his sentence.

Suddenly the end of lesson bell, which was welcomed by all the class, clanged with a sharp abrupt tone and the two boys made off to the rusty old bicycle sheds to unchain their means of manual transport.

"You go first, Oliver, and I'll follow you." The traffic that afternoon was deathly busy as it was a typical Monday afternoon, everyone all filling the roads and motorways to get home, deliver freight, to be in the pub or be with their families.

"I bet you haven't heard the latest release from Blur," quipped Oliver in a very dreary tone.

"Um, not to sure I've heard too much of them," replied Alex. "What, you've got to be kiddin', son . I'll show you the business!" As the two of them ran through the shopping precinct, they stopped to check their pockets to spend what they had from their paper rounds.

Boom! Boom! Boom! The rhythmic music beats pounded out their nightclub sound. As the two entered the megastore's black, darkly lit premises, they both began to keenly flick through all the plastic cases under the new release department.

"Don't bother with all that lot, absolute crap!"

"Do you use that sort of language when you're at home?"

Oliver just pulled a very arrogant grotesque face as if to say, "Does it matter anyway?"

The boy then headed over to the other rack and shouted, "Oasis are great but you've got to play it full blast to hear the full benefit."

Alex replied, "My dad likes Pete Townshend."

"Well, you'd better get used to it if you're gonna be in with the in crowd, talking of which are you feeling hungry? Ya, I know the bloke you're talking about, the tall lanky bloke with the big 'ooter!"

Alex looked somewhat lost by this time as he was used to music from his native country.

"I can't hear a word you're saying with all this noise in here."

"Well, yes, a bit," replied Alex above the noise of the shop.

"Fancy a KFC?" asked Oliver, changing the subject. "A what?" "You know, Kentucky Fried Chicken, the old bloke with the goatee whiskers."

Fifteen minutes later they handed over fistfuls of change to buy two piece meals for both of them.

"What's the time, Alex?" "Five forty five and it's time I started to get off home," he replied. Oliver frowned and they agreed that the two of them had better put in an appearance at their homes.

The busy A30 traffic was being diverted to all other routes around town, and as the two boys made their way to the High Street, all the pedestrian crossings became unusable as traffic stayed stationary with vehicles making their way to their final destinations.

"I know, let's cut across the road further up," Alex suggested as he waved his hand to his friend. The noise of the traffic drowned out their conversation as both of them searched for a gap in which they could cross over.

"Over here, Alex, you go first." Alex stepped off the pavement with his bicycle and made a straddled journey across the three lanes of traffic which led right up to the large Lightwater roundabout. Oliver followed on behind trying to catch up with Alex, with the lights changing from green to red and red back to green with monotonous frequency as the back of cars persistently flashed their stop lights.

"Hold on, Alex, bloody hell!" but Alex had become nervous and anxious as time was pressing on and the thought of a large reprimanding he would get from his family seemed more important than his company several yards behind. As he stepped off the central island, he paced his way in front of the cab of a curtain sided ten ton truck, the driver gunning his

71

engine as his full attention was on the cars in front of him, with the traffic lights changing in a mood of unreasonable sequences. Fortunately, Alex had walked clear of the truck cabin, but the driver had failed to notice Oliver following on behind as he sat in his high up seat. As the lights turned green, he threw his cigarette butt out of the window and let up his clutch pedal with full revs as the young impudent boy stepped in front of his radiator grille. The truck pounced forward in first gear dragging the young boy under its front wheels, with a crushing masticating noise of metal and grinding of human guts. Oliver went through the motions of desperately struggling and crying out but it was all over too quickly. His arms, chest and head gave a pathetic slapping sound as he disappeared under the front axles of the truck.

"Oliver!"

There was no reply as all that appeared in any form of an answer were several streams of blood that came from the truck's front end.

"Help, please help!" screamed Alex in a voice so high and desperate that his vocal cords just broke up. The driver, with a shocked, panic-stricken voice, leapt from the cab to give devastated appraisal of this unimaginable drama.

"Oh God, no!" Oh God, no!"

A bus queue of street gawpers turned their heads as they looked for comfort for this shocking sight as an elderly man shouted, "Somebody call an ambulance!" as a young lady dialed 999 on her mobile phone.

A great crowd of pedestrians gathered around the tragic scene as the driver cracked under the reality of it all and resigned himself to the fact that he had just killed a thirteen year old boy, by gently sitting himself on the kerb with his head in his hands and crying . A young lady in her twenties took pity on him and came forward from the staring crowd, sat down and put her arm around him.

Wow, wow, wow! as wailing emergency services sirens could be heard in the distance while Alex stood and stared with disbelief at the picture he saw in front of him.

"Come out of the way, lad, there' s nothing to see," said a Policeman's voice from behind him as his hand on his shoulder led him to the crowded and totally shocked pavement. Alex turned around slowly and obliged the man's command. A flashing police Land Rover edged its way down the blocked A road as its driver leapt from its seat like a western cowboy dismounting his horse.

"Everybody go, come on, it's all over. Go, move!" he shouted, waving his arms in a sweeping direction from side to side. The crowd slowly dispersed but those who remained regarding the all-important question. What sight lay under the truck?

"Get ready for this one, Ray, you can bet your arse this one's a goner!" The police driver tentatively climbed into the cab, slowly and timidly put it into reverse gear and slowly applied the gas pedal.

The engine roared as though it was a sleeping dragon that had awoken from its fiery slumbers. The policeman standing in front of the lorry slowly took his hand away from his eyes as he slowly viewed the mutilated corpse as it reappeared from under the front axle.

"God's strewth, well, he certainly couldn't have known much about it," slurred the PC as the decapitated chest of the victim gave the clear indication of the boy's death.

Chapter 12

"My God, this could have so easily been your son," wheezed Steve as he heard the frantic story upon Alex's return from Deepcut Police Station. Natalie looked totally transfixed and dumbstruck after two policemen had left after bringing Alex home. His mother just groaned in an emotionally charged voice.

"We've just got to get away from this place, Steve, we've got no choice."

Her husband sprang to his feet and embraced his wife.

"Its all closing in on us, I can't stand this any more. Let's get out of here before its too late!" screeched Natalie .

"I'd bloody love to, but how? I haven't got two pennies to rub together," snapped back Steve.

"It seems we are prisoners of this place, don't you see?"

Natalie began to become more traumatized by the events of that afternoon until Steve snapped, stormed out of the room and headed for the nearest pub, snorting and ranting as he slammed the door. In his mind he could see what was happening as the warning in the bathroom would come to reality. If he didn't defeat this menacing threat to his family's lives, then it would only be a matter of time until he would be a victim as well.

"Anytime, any place, anywhere, it's with us and watching us," he whispered to himself as he reached the top of the street. He was right. Steve came to a halt as though he was standing to attention at Trooping the Colour. The road was empty and quiet that evening as hardly any traffic could be heard. As he crossed the empty A road a hundred yards from his home he became eerily aware there was more sound around him than there should be. From behind he could hear a second pair of footsteps, sounding like Chelsea dealer boots.

"Jeepers," he whispered to himself as he glanced over his shoulder, only to notice that the only person that was there was a teenager some distance behind him.

"It can't be him," he thought as he increased his pace to a brisk walking speed. The footsteps got louder as he headed to the labyrinth of underpasses that led to the Cricketers pub, his favourite watering hole. His forehead sweated and his throat went dry as he tried to shake off the menacing footsteps that pursued him.

"Got it! I'll try and lose it at the next turning."

As he began a slow trot, the footsteps behind him made clacking noises like horses' hooves, between the two of them making the same rhythmic noise as Abba's "Take a Chance on Me" single. To his horror, from behind came a new sound like a tap dance from Broadway. As soon as he came to his chosen exit, he quickly turned right and threw himself against the wall, his heart pounding, awaiting his pursuer.

"Three, two, one!" he counted as he sprang from the darkness into the path of the entity that had been hard on his heels.

Thud! All that he experienced was as though somebody had run straight through him. A whole shoulder and chest went straight through his upper torso for a split second, as he was spent spinning to the ground in a sprawling heap.

"Urgghh, arrgghh, my God!" He looked all around him in totally dazed surprise. There was nobody there, just as it was before.

"Come out, wherever you are. For God's sake show yourself!"

There was total silence. Nothing. Steve cautiously clambered to his feet, brushing all the dust and muck off his office trousers.

"Phew," he gasped as he felt the chilly wind caress his body as he continued his way to the other end of the underpass to the pub to obtain refuge from the coldness he felt. With a firm push he opened the heavy oak door and dribbled his way through the crowded noisy tables until he found himself a space in the crowded bar. All those around greeted him with a hostile reception as one fat scruffy man wearing a Del Trotter style sheepskin jacket exclaimed.

"Gawd strewth, it's bloody freezing in 'ere all of a sudden. What the 'ell's 'append? Has the air conditioning started blowing out freezing cold air all of a sudden?"

His and his friends' attention started drifting towards Steve, who was still trying to get service from the heavily made up bar lady.

"I know this sounds really daft, Mike, but that cold draught seems to be coming from that office bod to your left."

"Yeah, you're most probably right, Dave, but it was OK before he came in."

Steve looked all around him and could see that his presence in the pub was causing an unwelcome stir with the customers. Within fifteen minutes he had downed a pint of Old Speckled Hen and was making his way back to his bungalow, not really feeling any better for his emergency drink, as the "Jack's Fish and Chips" neon sign grabbed his attention across the road. He didn't feel hungry yet his mind was unusually fired by the sight of roast chicken colour posters in the shop window.

"That's bloody strange, I don't usually like chip shop chicken."

As he opened the front door to the bungalow, his heart began to beat in an unusual aggressive manner, which was unlike his macho Mr Cool persona he had always maintained about himself.

Natalie stood there in the lounge with hardly a happy greeting.

"Alex has gone to bed. If you're going out in future you can at least take your coat with you. You're freezing cold."

Steve just stood there gritting his teeth and decided not to mention anything about his unusual encounter in the subway.

"Your supper's in the oven, goulash, dumplings and vegetables. I want a bath tonight so you'll just have to serve yourself."

Steve just replied with some apprehension from his abrupt wife, but when he came to put his arms around her, she just pushed him away.

"My God, you're like a block of ice."

Steve was totally confused as his wife had always greeted him with traditional hugs and kisses.

"All right then, I'll serve myself."

He just looked at the plate and thought, "I'm not in the mood for this crap." He just dumped it on the table and the exhaustion of the day's events began to grip his mind and body by falling asleep on the sofa. As he lay there curled up on the three seater, a grim disturbing vision came into his mind. He was in an HM Prison cell and was awoken at 2.00 am. It was 23 February 1947. Three men stood by his Spartan prison bed and ordered him to stand up.

"On your feet, Wheeler," growled a prison warder, wearing typical black uniform and cap. As the heavy iron door slammed behind him, he was led along the landing to a small room at the far end of the prison. His blindfold was removed with a fast tug and there in front of him was a firm rope noose. At this point, Steve awoke and glanced up at the clock at the far end wall. It was 1.15 am.

"Bollocks, and I've got to be at work tomorrow."

As he wiped and scratched his face he realized, "my God, I feel so cold," as he shivered on the sofa without any blankets. After smacking his teeth in a very loud manner, he staggered into the bathroom to brush his teeth. As he switched on the mirror light he saw his ashen reflection in front of him, his complexion having a mask-like, deathly look about it.

"Maybe it was just the strain of the dreadful day that had a lot to do with it."

After he finished his ablutions he crept into bed beside his wife, who was snoring heavily on her side.

Chapter 13

"Everything all right, Steve?" enquired his colleague as he wandered into the office just before the 9.00 am signal came up on his desk digital clock.

"Nah, mate."

"Why, what's up?" he persisted as he tentatively sipped a plastic cup of Nescafe from the company drinks machine. There was a very harsh silence as he banged his briefcase down on the table.

"The boy's mate was killed under a lorry last night as he came home from school and it seems that he will have to go to court and give evidence on how it all happened."

"Bloody 'ell, this one's going to be a big 'un. How'd all this happen?"

"Oh, the whole thing was just bloody stupid!"

"What ya mean bloody stupid?"

"Look, for God's sake, it just bloody happened, alright!"

Steve went silent. What had come over him? He was usually quite well mannered and calm but since the previous evening in the underpass he seemed to feel threatened, vulnerable and above all aggressive.

"Flaming 'ell you look pale . Are you feeling OK, mate?"

"No, mate, I feel that I'm not in control of myself. I had this really bad dream last night as though I was about to be hanged for murder."

"I think you should take some time off, mate, you're looking really stressed out."

"Look, Don, just drop it will ya. It's none of your business, alright!"

Don just sat there totally astonished as the Steve he saw in front of him was not the same Steve he had known for the last two years. He had never heard him get so annoyed and grumpy in such a short space of time; his mannerisms were of a persona who felt threatened and paranoid. Don just lowered his eyes until all he could see was the keyboard of his PC terminal. Steve strutted to the filing cabinet to search for the Hochiki costing file and after a long fickle find eventually found it, slammed the drawer shut with a loud bang and then hurled it across the office onto his desk. All that followed was a very sinister silence. Don could see that he was like a bomb about to explode with a very defective detonator. As the other colleagues came in they sensed that there was some thing wrong and gave Steve's desk a very wide berth.

Beep, beep, beep went the telephone on his desk. "Hello, sales," he replied.

"I've got Toshiba for you."

"Oh, put it through," he groaned.

"Hello, is that you, Steve? Two weeks ago I advised you by email that a ton of printers was for temporary import. Why haven't I had that five grand refunded from Customs yet?" whinged the client on the other end of the line.

"Well, how am I supposed to know that, you stupid plonker?" Steve growled in a very fiery offhand tone.

The line went very quiet for ten seconds and then there was a loud clunk as the receiver was put down the other end. Five minutes later, Steve's boss, Paul Carpenter, came charging into the room and came to an abrupt halt in front of his desk.

"Steve, Steve, what have you said to Chris Coombe?"

"Look, pal, I haven't got a crystal ball. How am I supposed to flaming know?"

"Come into my office immediately," in a tone that spelled out that he was in serious trouble.

"If you've got something to say you can bloody well tell me here and now."

"Go home, Steve."

"Bugger off, you great fat pillock!"

"Steve, pack your bags and go home. You are suspended until further notice."

"I'm not moving."

"If you don't go home now I will call the police."

That was the final straw of the argument. As soon as Steve heard the word 'police' he sprang to his feet and barked in Paul's face, "Don't you ever say that word to me, Paul, or I'll bloody well deck ya."

"You'll do what?" replied Paul with his eyes popping out like organ stops.

"I'll bloody kill ya."

Then, like a tiger, he thrust both hands at Paul's throat, pushing his thumbs against his windpipe.

"Oh my God!" screamed the director's secretary as three other members of staff leapt to the rescue of the threatened man. They dragged Steve to the floor, pinning his arms to his side away from Paul's face like a scene from the Sweeney.

"Somebody call the police!"

"No, that won't be necessary!"

The secretary ran out to the warehouse to fetch help from the burly, chunkiest warehouse men that were off-loading the back of an articulated truck. Steve was held in an arm lock, forced down the stairs and hurled from the office reception area into the car park where he was ordered, "Don't come back, you're fired for gross misconduct!"

Steve stood there in full view of his colleagues, feeling total embarrassment with a degraded conscience. As he sped off out the car park with his cam belt slipping with a screeching noise, the events of the past hour suddenly hit him.

"My God, what have I done, what am I going to do now? I've never done anything like this before in my life!" Suddenly it all made sense as he realized what had happened the night before in the underpass. When he jumped out to confront his pursuer, the malignant spirit ran straight into him and came to rest deep within his soul, with its aggressive impulse and total paranoia behind the wheel of Steve's mind. Steve was possessed. The time was now 10.17 am and most of the day was still ahead of him as he retuned home with his heart beating, his forehead sweating and his mouth snarling like a tiger.

As he opened the door he could tell that nobody was at home, just as he had expected. What was he to do now? He was now jobless. How could he explain this to his wife? Would she now leave him and divorce him? His mind restlessly turned over and over until he could take no more. He slumped on the bed with an exasperated sensation in his body, and drifted off to sleep. As he lay there he had a similar vision to the one he had the night before. As he walked along a prison landing, a few fellow inmates challenged him and a scuffle broke out with him pushing a prisoner over the banister rail, his face screaming with hysteria as he finally hit the bottom four seconds later with an unforgettable loud thud. The noise in his mind woke him as he queried the phenomenon as to why he had a dream about prison drama.

Klinkle, rattle, clank. The sound of the front door lock broke the eerie silence as Steve had to suddenly snap out of his sinister dream. He knew it was Alex returning from school and of course he would be asking as to why he was home so early from work. Steve breathed in and counted his paces as he eventually walked into the bedroom.

"Hello, Alex, come in."

"Steve, why aren't you at work?" he replied in an innocent

but knowing tone that made his stepfather go silent for many moments.

"Oh, well, I had some time owing to me as holiday so I thought I'd take a half day as there wasn't much doing and I haven't any appointments today."

Alex looked at him in doubt as to whether he was telling the truth or not. He knew that he was a workaholic that did not give up easily as he would usually stay to the end to finish a job. As he walked around the lounge shuffling his feet, the young boy became aware that something was wrong and asked, "Do you know when mum will be home as I want to have my dinner and go out with Matt."

He was stuck for an answer as he knew that he still had to explain to his wife what had happened that morning. His real explanation would be totally impossible to explain that he had throttled a senior manager.

"I'm just going out for a while, lad, I've got some shopping to do."

"OK sure. I'll see you later," came the reply in a very quiet tone.

As he made his way to the recruitment agency in the High Street, his whole body and mind began to quiver and convulse with a certain anger that was unbeknown to him. Certain flashes of a man's previous life flicked into his mind and certain characters that were dressed in 1940's style clothes seemed to occupy his sense of memory as he clenched his fingers into a fist to get a hold of himself.

"I'm possessed by a spirit and it's taking over my mind and body. Only my soul is fighting back against it." He kept repeating over and over in his mind, "I am Steve Harrison, born 31 August 1959 in Balham, South London." After every eighth time he repeated this he received a jolting sensation.

"You are Jack Wheeler of Stepney, East London, born 5 March 1912."

"Get out of my mind, Jack, I am Steve Harrison."

"Don't fight me, Steve, I will have you."

"No! You will not have me, Jack, I am Steve Harrison."

As he reached the top of the stairs that lead to SW Staff Bureau, he met a man in his late forties with an Irish accent.

"Have you made an appointment, sir?"

To Steve this was an unwelcome reception and he replied, "Today I've lost my job at Heathrow. I've twenty one years experience in the freight forwarding industry and import export logistics. Do you have any suitable vacancies on your books?"

"Hmm … sometimes happens," replied the proprietor.

"Well, first things first, please fill out this agency questionnaire and well see what we have in store."

As Steve sat behind an empty desk he struggled with all the questions involved. Now and then he glanced at Dan, only to be given doubtful a frosty expression in return. After fifteen minutes he handed the form back to him. Dan browsed through it and said, "Now, you were with AVS Logistics for the past two years and now you've had your membership terminated. Well, it would be easier to get you placed in a job if you hadn't been fired." Suddenly Steve felt a jolt of aggression thrash through his body at this remark and felt provoked to lash out at the Irishman's throat, but he managed to restrain himself.

"Well, I'll do my best, er … Steve, but it will be a bit tricky to match your salary that you were on."

"Sounds bloody promising," thought Steve as he zipped up his BMW anorak.

Upon his return journey he became more and more convinced that his registration had been a complete waste of time.

"Well, nothing ventured, nothing gained," he groaned to himself as he turned his key in the front door only to be confronted by his wife, Natalie, her face steaming with anger to the point of exploding.

"Your office has been on the phone. What's going on, Steven? Why have you come home so early? Have you been told they don't want you?"

"What did they say, Natalie?"

"You're to call the office immediately."

Steve stared at the telephone for a few seconds, biting his bottom lip, and then he reached out slowly and dialed the office number . He was put through to the MD's secretary who firmly told him, "Please return all company property and collect your personal effects first thing tomorrow morning." He then put the receiver down and looked at his wife.

"What's happened?" Natalie asked.

"Oh, eh, got a problem at the office."

"What problem?"

"I've got to have a meeting with them tomorrow morning."

"Steve, you're lying to me."

"Look, dear, I've just been kicked out of my company!"

"Kicked out! Why, what have you done?"

"I had a bloody row with the commercial manager, you know, that dickhead that I've been moaning about for ages. Where ever you go, Natalie, you always get these dickhead people."

"Wherever you have worked, Steven, you've had these dickhead people. So what are you going to do now?" Natalie added with a totally unimpressed lack of confidence voice.

"You've lost your job, now how do you think you are going to get paid?"

"I've just registered at SW Staff and they can get me an interview by the end of the week."

"So what's going to happen when you tell them that you got the sack?"

"I'll think of something, I always do," replied Steve in a tired, nervous 'don't add to my troubles' tone.

"Oh, so you've had the sack before, is this true?"

"Everyone gets the sack at some time in their lives, Natalie."

"Well, I've never had it," Natalie snapped.

"Look, for bloody hell's sake, woman, will you just bloody belt up!"

Steve suddenly snapped and he began to search the room for something to strike his wife with.

"My God, Steve, what's the matter with you?" he thought to himself.

"I seem to be possessed by a mind of social violence. This is most unlike me."

He fought back against his physical actions as Natalie began to crouch down in the corner of the lounge waiting for her husband to strike her. Not a word passed between them as Steve grabbed his coat and stormed out of the lounge to his car. Alex, in the meantime, had taken cover in his bedroom under the bed. "Its alright, Alex, you can come out now."

"What's going on, mum?"

"I don't think this is all Steven's fault what has happened. It's all something to do with this horrible home . It's all been a big mistake. I think we have upset some lost souls of the past and they want to break us as a family. It's all to do with this place we've bought. I know I didn't tell you this but a month after we moved in I had a dream that I was stripping off the wallpaper in the bedroom and there on the wall underneath were the figures 666. I had a feeling that this dream was a message telling us to be aware that this home had satanic connections. It's all come true, Alex . Whatever is here wants us out of the way. It wants to kill us all. As I remember, what I was told in the book of Revelations was that Satan comes out of the earth and had two horns. Any image of the Devil bore

86

the figures 666 on his right hand or forehead. I can see what's happening now. The power of Satan is trying to force us from this place."

The Volvo V40 sped down the London Road A30, the driver sat behind the wheel, his mind and body pumping with stress and adrenaline to the sound of UFO's "Lights Out" song.

"Wind blows back with the batons charging
It winds all the way, right to the butt of my gun.
Maybe now your time has come."

His thoughts and emotions kept sticking to his memories of his teens when he frequented the Hammersmith Odeon to all the various hard rock acts.

The hypnotic rhythm of the chorus echoed through his mind until he reached the office of his terminated employment. *Clunk* as he slowly and tentatively pushed his company ID and effects through the letterbox in a such a way as to make a farewell gesture. The atmosphere suddenly went all very eerie as he stood back from the office doorstep and admired his reflection in the glass pane with the moonlight behind him.

"Good evening, sir. Can I ask you what you are doing here at this hour?"

Steve looked over his shoulder and there at the complex gate was a white police Ford Granada, with a burly PC climbing out of the driver's side and walking towards him.

"Oh, don't worry, Sir, I can explain. I am returning my company pass and credentials," replied Steve in a very light-hearted tone. The officer did not reply. He just stared at him until he eventually dropped his eyes.

"Well, as soon as you can, would you and your colleague in the car be so kind as to be off the premises immediately. As you know you are on CCTV camera so for whatever reason this company can have a legal issue with you." Steve shuddered and went very pale like a large tub of emulsion paint.

"Oh God, please God, no," he thought to himself. He knew immediately what this meant as he looked at the passenger seat and all he could see was an empty car. The situation he was in was one of duress, to get in the car and drive off without any argument. He slowly strutted to the driver's door and very gingerly started the engine.

"Good night, officer."

The PC just stared back at him with a 'Do I have to tell you twice' expression on his face. Steve just pulled out of the driveway as the police car followed him on his journey back to the London A30.

"Shit! Shit! Shit! What's that?" as he felt tingling all over the top of his scalp. An icy finger stroked his nose and cheek and then suddenly stopped.

"Just ignore it," he thought to himself as the police car behind him took a right turn and disappeared from sight. The sound inside the car went totally and deathly silent as he could faintly hear the sound of his own breathing. As he drove towards Colnbrook his heart began to beat more strongly as he flicked the left indicator to take the first turning of the large cargo terminal roundabout. Sweat poured from his brow as his steering wheel refused to turn to the left despite the use of power assisted steering and his strong vice-like grip on the wheel.

"Oh God, no!" His mind was not naive enough to realize what lay ahead. In the dead of night the car sped on in a westwards direction to the King George reservoir where scrub field gave accommodation for lonely horses close to Datchet.

"Try the radio," he thought as his nervous fingers reached out for the power button. The green light lit up but despite adjusting the volume control, the sound stayed very silent. Then the worst happened.

Clunk! the central locking locked into place as he became a prisoner in his own car. In the darkness of the country road, the car lost its way in a district without street lights.

"Take the road to the left, its bound to lead to Windsor!" His face began to contort with fear and emotion as his eyes began to fill up with panicking tears. *Sniff, sniff* as he tried to breathe through his nose that was full of wet snot.

Bump! Bang! Clang! went his wheels and suspension as the car went over a deep muddy hole in a lost country lane.

"Bloody hell, no, I'm in a bloody farmer's field, turn left and get out of here!" But as he frantically steered the car, it came to a lethargic stop as it ran into a muddy bog. *Vroooooom* the engine sounded as Steve slammed his foot on the gas pedal, sending the car skidding hopelessly down a bank to the edge of a gravelly stream.

Thud, bang! as the engine stalled to indicate that his car journey had come to an untimely end. With his desperate panting breath, he lay sprawled across the passenger seat caused by the impact of the car crashing at an awkward angle.

"Come on, Harrison, pull yourself together, mate," he groaned to himself as he reached for the electric car window switch to release himself from the trap he was in.

"Yes, yes, yes!" he cried as the glass shield operated itself and a gust of pig manure came in through the new gap. As he tried to pull himself out, his hand slipped and the window wound itself back up again, trapping his neck and shoulders in a scissor like operation.

"Arrgghh, flaming hell, help … help! I'm over here!" he screamed frantically in the loneliness of the pitch black field. Nobody came. Suddenly a tall man in his mid-twenties wearing an old grey denim uniform appeared from round the back of the car, his face stiff and wooden like with a satisfied expression around his mouth.

"Bloody 'ell, mate, you're an answer to prayer," said Steve in a very jolly relieved voice.

The man just stood there looking at him head on with his arms folded.

"Well, can you undo the door and get me out of here?"

The man just looked at Steve in total silence as though he was deaf and his face of cold stone, then a moment later he flexed his arms and stretched his fingers as though he was contemplating the next move. Suddenly he shuffled his feet and then ran off into the darkness. "Hell, there's something not right about that bloke. Perhaps his ESN or something odd," Steve whispered to himself.

A few minutes later he returned with a slow stroll to his stride with a large lump of wood shaped like a club. Steve's face dropped from his rescued expression.

"I'm sorry, mate, but as you can see I'm stuck, can you get me out of here?" he said, trying to be polite but at the same time trying to get his desperate message across. The man's face started to contort and then he slowly lifted the club above his head as though he was about to ring the bell and win a prize at the fair ground.

Thwack as it came down across Steve's left temple. It happened all too quickly. His forehead was gashed by the blow, blood oozing like a burst blood vessel from his face.

Thwack! The club struck him again, this time across his nose and cheek. His face turned into a river of blood as it streamed down his nostrils and cheeks and into his mouth. Steve looked up at his attacker as his voice gurgled with the mixture of all liquids in his throat and croaked,

"Go on, kill me, for what's my life worth, kill me!"

The man's face broke into a cruel, wicked smile like a crazed schizophrenic, then suddenly he delivered the final blow that would knock him half unconscious. His head hung from the jammed car window like a horse from its stable hatch. With a gleeful expression on his face, the attacker ran towards an area of field where refuse was disposed of, and returning with an oily sack which he threw over Steve's head to act as an execution mask. After freeing his head, his body was dragged silently from the driver's seat by his legs, his voice silently gurgling his last words, "Natalie … wife …family."

Nobody came. Nobody could hear the voice of this last tragic scene.

Shhhhh … Shhhhhhh … Shhhhhhhhh as his body was dragged face upwards, his anorak dragging on the wet grass, while his blood-filled throat gurgled out words from his semi-conscious, delirious mind.

"Harggghhh … harggghhh," as he struggled to breathe, with his hands reaching and searching in the darkness for help which did not come, the trees by the edge of the field swishing in reply to hide his last effort to attract help. As he lay by the edge of the stony gravel pit, his accomplice had found a new weapon, a large dirty breeze block, to finish off his defenceless victim.

Thud! Crack! Crush! as for the third time the 18 pound rock smashed down onto Steve's face, and this time there were no more cries for help from under the oily sack. A heavy stream of blood flowed through the filthy cloth where his nose was. The murderer got to his feet and with a sickly smirk, knew what this meant. Steve, his victim, was dead. The husband and father of the young family lay there totally still, the only human flesh showing his mud and grass stained hands that peeped innocently from the sleeves of his BMW anorak. The figure in old grey stood with a Napoleonic pose in front of his victim, then turned and disappeared into the night.

"Have you heard from Steven yet?" asked Alex as Natalie chewed her right thumb nail and shook her head, all very tearful.

"Perhaps I should call the police now," she whispered, brushing back a tear as the clock on the chimney breast struck twelve o'clock. She slowly wandered across the lounge as though she was hoping for the telephone to ring just in time. Picking up the receiver she slowly dialed 999 and five seconds later the operator answered the call.

"Emergency services, police, fire or ambulance?"

"Oh hello, oh … police please."

"Police, putting you through now."

"Hello, Surrey Police."

"Oh, good evening, Natalie Harrison, I want to report that my husband has gone missing."

"I see, madam, and what's his name and address?"

Natalie replied in an emotional whisper, giving her postcode as well.

"Right, madam, can you give me a full description and his age, and his car registration number as well if he was driving a car at the time of his disappearance?". The officer sounded very matter of fact, not showing any emotion or sympathy with Natalie. After fifteen minutes she put the receiver down and nervously prepared herself for bed, her dry stiff tongue making it a problem for her to clean her teeth. As she lay in bed, the suspense became too much for her. Eventually she turned over and fell asleep as the Sony radio alarm clock flicked away the night on its LED display.

Chapter 14

The driver's door of the Ford Orion slammed shut as the middle aged woman in her green zip up rain mac released her German shepherd dog from the rear of her car. The Alsatian leaped across the open grass as though it had been paroled on good behaviour, its nose sniffing the air in search of a possible meal. Its pace increased to full charge as it noticed a silver Volvo estate close to the water's edge.

"Jazz! Jazz! Come here!" The dog did not return as its curiosity was drawn to a shadowy figure lying without any claimant. The dog licked its hand and wrist that was deathly cold and then returned to its owner.

"What have you found, boy? I don't care what it is just as long as it's a good bag of cash!"

The dog sped off again, over the ridge and down the other side with its owner trotting after it.

"Oh my God!" The woman stopped dead in her tracks as though she was rooted to the ground.

"Hello, my name is Natalie Harrison. I rang yesterday evening about my missing husband, has there been any more news?"

There was a stone cold silence as though the Police officer knew something of a grave nature. "Ehhhhh … no."

"Are you sure?"

"I'm expecting a report back from last night's shift. Until then I can't say if I have any news."

"I see, OK then, goodbye."

She slowly replaced the receiver and glanced at the clock on the video recorder. It read 10.19 as she wandered into the kitchen to switch the electric kettle on. *Bzzzzzzz* went the front doorbell. Natalie's face went a dull ashen colour as a chilling sensation went down her back to her legs.

"Oh God," she thought. "Is this going to be the bad news that I am expecting?"

AS Natalie answered the door she was met by two police constables, one a stocky man with a beard and the other a small WPC wearing her police battle bowler.

"Is this the home of Steven Harrison of Harley Meadows that was reported missing last night by his wife Natalie Harrison?" "Yes, you are correct."

The policeman breathed in slowly and deeply and he knew he had to break tragic news to the attractive woman standing in her dressing gown with the front door open.

"This is Surrey Police about your missing husband. The car registration you gave last night has been recovered from an area of scrub land in Datchet. Before we go any further, can you come to Ashford Hospital to formally identify the body that is being held there?"

"What do you mean … a body. Is this my husband or not?"

"Well, we are not sure if the body found is your husband's, but we need you to confirm as to who this is. This particular one has some very bad facial injuries as though it has been struck by a large rock of some sort."

Natalie's face grimaced and twitched at what she heard and then she quickly got dressed, put on her coat from the hallway cupboard and followed the two PCs to their Panda car.

"Yes, that's Steven," as the mortuary assistant pulled back the hospital covers that revealed her husband's badly crushed face.

"You're quite sure?" asked the officer.

"Yes," replied Natalie in a croaky, heartbroken voice.

After she was given an hour to console herself, Natalie was then led away to the mortuary manager's office and was given permission to use the telephone.

"Can you explain your husband's last hours?" asked a plain dressed police detective.

"The last time I saw him was at 8.45 pm last night to return some equipment to his company that he had just left. He said that he would return in about an hour, but he never returned and I never heard any more. There had been a row at the office that day but he seemed in control of himself."

"I see," said the inspector.

"It goes without saying that we need to make a report on all the DNA involved, so when you are ready we need to take your fingerprints so we can match those on the car and the items at the scene of the murder."

"OK," replied Natalie in a not so confident voice.

"Do you now of any people that would want to murder your husband?"

"No, we always attracted good company. Steve was a mature, intelligent man, that's all I can say."

"Right, well, can you come to Staines Police Station tomorrow afternoon at two o'clock to make a full statement and give DNA records along with your son?"

Natalie agreed and was driven back to her home and in her typical Slavic way she stood composed and totally still by the lounge window, not blinking or moving a muscle for an hour until her son knocked on the door. Alex didn't need to ask what had happened as her face said it all as he was ushered inside.

"It's all very strange indeed," remarked the inspector of the CID. "We've checked all the fingerprints on the door handles of your husband's car and all they show are yours, your husband's and your son's. All the DNA on the upholstery has also been checked and it doesn't show anybody else's other than that of your family. Are you sure you weren't there on the night of your husband's murder?"

"Yes, of course I am sure!" snapped Natalie, totally astonished by the policeman's remark.

"In that case, Mrs Harrison, I suggest we discuss the night of your husband's death in further detail. Can you step this way please?"

After a further ninety minutes, they came to the same conclusion as they did the day before.

"Now then, Mrs Harrison, can you please describe the condition of your marriage just before Steven was … killed phwwwwwww?"

There was a stony silence as Natalie struggled to describe the events of the last six months.

"It seems that you had troubles at home culminating in your husband getting the sack, only it seems that your life does not sound at all settled, Mrs Harrison. Are you meeting somebody this evening, Mrs Harrison?"

"Yes, my son is coming home from school at three thirty and my friend is coming round as well."

"Well, I suggest you call your friend and tell her to collect your son from school or your home. I think you will be here for some time until we really get to the bottom of this. All that you have told us has many flaws and all sounds too flimsy."

The scenario of that night was thrashed out yet again.

"Right, Mrs Harrison, there is not enough evidence to convict you of murdering your husband."

"You thought that I had murdered my husband?"

"There is not enough evidence to suggest that you had taken part in his death, but we will of course now be making further investigations."

"You callous pig!" hissed Natalie as she grabbed her shoulder bag and coat.

"Just a minute, I haven't said you can go. You are to be

detained for an indefinite period until you are able to prove to us that you were not present at the scene of your husband's murder."

Natalie went a totally pale colour and sank back into her sparsely padded office seat, but was soon given a cup of weak station tea by the WPC on duty at the reception desk outside. After signing the signature line on the police statement she was lead away to the cells to the very ground floor, her mind in sheer dismay as her belt and any long personal effects were taken from her and put in a safe box.

"Yes, I can confirm that Mrs Natalie Harrison was at her home between the hours of eight pm to eight am on the night of 10 October 1993. I called around to her home to return some garments that I had altered for her. She did explain to me that her husband had returned to his office earlier that evening due to some unexplained issues at his place of work." After the formalities were submitted to the inspector in question, Natalie was united with her friend, Lena Hookway, who had been her old neighbour when she first arrived in England.

"Lena, thank God you're here," Natalie sighed so loudly that the whole building was aware of the reception drama. An hour later she was home, hoping that she would wake up and the past forty-eight hours had just been a ghastly nightmare. It wasn't. As she fell asleep on her small double bed, the empty space beside her reminded her of her late husband's absence with the police letter folded and crumpled on the bedside table.

It took a full twelve days for the Surrey Police Constabulary to complete their full investigations. Due to an adamant witness and lack of evidence, Natalie was not convicted of murdering her husband Steve and her name was removed from the suspect list.

"It's OK, Lena, I can manage," replied Natalie as the black hearse pulled up silently outside the lounge windows. As the small party slowly marched out of the front door they all glanced upwards to view the light oak coffin that was proudly and neatly decorated in the shiny black vehicle that was to transport the mourners to the church. The atmosphere was of complete shock and disbelief that all the events of the last twelve months would lead to this.

"Mum, do you think you will get married again?" asked Alex in a very hopeful optimistic tone.

His mother just turned her head in his direction and gave a slight cough with an indication of acknowledgement to her son. When the motorcade of black cars turned into the church car park, members of the clergy were waiting outside with their faces dictating that during the following hour, humour and social enjoyment would be forbidden. Steve's father looked on the bright Cockney side as he remarked to his remaining son.

"The retiring collection should be blooming good judging by the number of people that have turned out."

As the pall bearers sedately lifted the coffin from the back of the hearse, silent footsteps led the procession inside the church. A large number took their seats in total stony silence, as most awaited the grim reality of what had to be told, while Steve's family followed the coffin down the aisle confirming the truth of his murder. The whole service lasted about thirty minutes as a closing hymn indicated a tragically solemn closing, but even more so there was a challenging matter on Natalie's mind.

What was she to do now? Stay in England or move back to the Ukraine? Even more challenging, from the evidence that the police had put together, her husband's murder was no ordinary murder. Whatever force that did it would most probably be interested in her and her son, Alex.

"Take my advice, Natalie, get yourself back to where you belong in the Ukraine. Your whole life is cursed in this country, you just don't belong here," whispered Lena.

"Maybe you're right, my whole life has become absolute

hell from the first month I came here. This place just isn't my home. Before I moved here I had a perfectly settled life. It seems I could sell the bungalow and buy a good flat in Vinnitsa."

As soon as she got home, Natalie decided to do what all women do when they are trying to block out trouble and pain from their minds. "Make yourself as busy as possible" was the name of the game. She totally re-arranged the bedroom so that her bed was the opposite way around and with the new silence in the home. The more she felt it, the harder she worked. Totally exhausted, she undressed and ran herself a steaming hot bath.

Splosh ... Splash. Despite all the unexpected things that happen in life, certain rituals still remain the same. As she dried herself off, she stood staring at herself in the full length mirror in the lounge, with her radiant fresh natural beauty showing through, similar to the Polish actress Joanna Kanska. As she lifted her wet fringe with her right finger, she stared at herself deep into her eyes and did the unthinkable. Her mind drifted back in her life when she was a student at Kharkov University. The eternity ring she wore when she graduated still gleamed on her left finger. The early nineties were tough years both for the USSR as well as for England. It was for these reasons that Steve and Natalie had a very mutual bond which brought them to marry and work for a better future. She divorced her first husband when she was twenty five on the grounds of his infidelity over an affair with a female work colleague. Upon meeting Steve on a tour when he was visiting old World War II battle sites with his cousin, she took the very difficult decision to leave her elderly mother, move to England on a fiancé visa and get married at Weybridge Registry Office. On her arrival, she found it difficult to adjust to England, the British reserve being the most difficult of all barriers to overcome. Where she had lived before for so many years, she had so many friends from her early years since she trained as a ballroom dancer with her own dance partner. Everyone who saw them perform assumed they were boy and girlfriend but that was not the case. By sheer coincidence she met a young man, Siroja, at the local town hall disco one Saturday night. He pestered and nagged her all evening for a date, but she was not interested. Her negative responses to his persistent advances did not deter him from giving up. It was only until the last half hour that she finally gave in to his offer of a night out to the theatre and a drink. They dated for a week and Siroja promised Natalie a good future and a secure happy life. It seemed a very inviting good proposal, especially as his father was the director of the local electricity company, with their own detached house with two German cars, not the usual Russian Volga. Natalie's elder sister advised her to marry him but she was not entirely convinced he was right for her. Siroja was an only child and seemed somewhat moody and spoiled when he didn't get his own way. Sure enough, after a month since they first met, he proposed. As all of her friends were getting married in their early twenties, she took the advice and accepted and they were married in the Church Of St Nicholai in Vinnitsa. It was a great ceremony with over a hundred guests, but it seemed apparent afterwards why so many guests had turned up. The reception was a buffet meal and those that were invited went for the food like a pack of wolves. It was an occasion full of mixed emotions, especially as Natalie's father had not approved of Siroja. His attitude had not met with her father's approval. He was reluctant to go along with his daughter's marriage to him and clearly felt that his new son-in-law was not right for his daughter. He was to be proved right within the first year of their marriage. After their honeymoon on the Black Sea, the two of them moved into Natalie's parents' flat as they were unable to find an appropriate apartment for themselves. Natalie was working at the machine building plant as an accountant and Siroja was working as an electrical contractor. He had shown disappointment with his new in-laws' home and as the commitment and work effort required to keep the marriage happy became too much, all romance seemed to go out of the window. For a while, the new life came to a deadlock, until Natalie arrived home from the local hospital one morning and announced she was pregnant. By all first accounts it was proved to be a girl until nine months later all their assumptions were dashed.

"It's a boy!"

"A boy?"

"Yes, look!"

"But I've bought all baby girl's clothes," whinged Natalie's mother.

"Well, don't worry, mum, he'll wear them until he soon grows out of them."

Later that week, Siroja came home from the registrar's office and made an announcement.

"We'll call him Alexander," holding a birth certificate with the boy's name on it.

"What!" exclaimed everyone.

"But we decided on Nazarei!"

"No, no, no, Alex sounds ten times better," proclaimed Siroja.

"You never said anything to me about this," snapped Natalie.

Siroja didn't answer. His facial expression said it all.

"I did what I think is right."

The next few moments were so intense that one could cut the atmosphere with a knife as it was all clear to see that the marriage was one big mistake. In the eighteen months that passed since their wedding, the young naïve couple had unresolvable differences and were in no doubt incompatible.

"You're late tonight, problems at work?" enquired Natalie to her husband as he came through the front door at 8.15. There was a stony silence as he shuffled his feet and did not take off his coat, which was quite unusual. Natalie soon latched on that there was something wrong, that he did not come home full of bitter criticism and chauvinistic orders and expectations.

"It's over, Natalie."

"What?" she queried.

"Our marriage … it's over, I've found another woman and I'm going now."

Natalie just sat in the kitchen totally transfixed and stunned by these last words. "Who is this woman?" she replied in a complete melodramatic voice.

"Valentina," he whispered.

"Valentina! It would have to be that two faced bitch!"

Natalie quickly resigned herself to the fact that her husband had had an affair with her old school friend and without any further ado he reached above the pine bedroom wardrobe, brought down his suitcases and began packing his personal effects. Within two hours he had loaded everything in the back of his car and left without saying so much as a goodbye, leaving his abandoned wife totally stunned with her head in hands, half sobbing at the kitchen table. The only luck for Siroja was that his mother-in-law was not at home to give her wayward son-in-law a good taste of her rolling pin that she kept by the front door.

As Natalie lay in bed that night, her mind was in absolute turmoil as she tossed from side to side.

It was that hunted feeling that came from within.

"Wake up, Natalie! Wake up!" came an alarm call from inside her mind. She turned to ignore it and insisted that she got a good night's sleep, but the warning message kept on like a telephone that would not stop ringing.

"Alright, I'll wake up," came the answer, and she gradually opened her eyes to see the reason for this mysterious call. In the silence of the bedroom just beside her pillow stood a five foot black figure wearing the same black cloak as before with a large pointed face with a black pointed nose which covered most of the front of its head. It stood there staring at her in the same position as it did when it gave its first appearance to her late husband. Three seconds later it turned sideways and then slipped through the wall. Natalie watched in total astonishment but this was hardly the first time this had happened.

"Oh shit, not again. After all that's happened to me I thought it would have left me alone by now!" she thought in her heartbroken mind. In her desperate mood, she rolled back to face the other direction and put her hands together to say the Lord's prayer.

"Dear God, what do I do now?"

She knew that with her husband gone, she had more pressure on her shoulders to pay the bills and for her son's welfare.

"Now look, Natalie, I'll have a word with the recruitment department and we'll most probably have a vacancy in accounts." Natalie's friend, Lena, had invited her over for the evening and tried to convince her that she should upgrade her job to work for Andrew's Balantyne Commodity Brokers in Woking.

"We pay twelve pounds per hour with regular overtime at weekends, Sundays pay double time so that should boost your income and there is also flexi-time available so you can see Alex at a reasonable hour."

"Sounds like good news, Lena, tell them that I'd be more than interested."

"Fine, tell you what, I'll let you know by the end of the week. You need money from now on, Natalie, Steve's not around anymore. You're on your own, girl!"

Lena's voice hurt her deeply but she knew she was right. Another worry on her mind was the black angelic being she had seen two nights before. She had decided not to tell anyone about this as she tried to inspire good optimism and not more doom and gloom that she got herself known for.

"My God, I hope I'm safe," she whispered.

Two weeks later there was a clutter and slap from her letter box as she was drying her face in the bathroom mirror.

"Yes!" she shrieked as she read the awaited letter aloud. "Dear Mrs Harrison, as per your recent interview with our Accounts Manager, Jennifer Westwood, we have pleasure in confirming your position as accounts payable controller. Your starting salary will be £16,000 per annum."

The letter ended with the usual sentence, "We look forward to seeing you on 3 November."

All she had to do now was to hand in her notice at Marks and Spencer. That evening she snatched the Basildon Bond writing pad from the sideboard and slowly wrote her name and address in the top right hand corner.

"Well, I hope this goes down OK," she uttered as she signed the bottom and wrote out the envelope to the HR department.

"Hmmmmm, if things don't work out, then give us a call," whinged Jackie, her floor manager, as she broke the news In a long winded scenario the following morning.

"You're still invited to the Christmas do," she added in a cheerful tone.

"Oh, don't worry, I'm still coming. Free food and no washing up, too good to miss!"

She felt better that the awkward news had now been broken and was feeling very optimistic she might even meet a new man at her new job. Her marriage to Steve had certainly had its rocky times and there might now be a time for happier memories.

"Hello, Alex, how did school go? Did you get any good feedback on the art homework?"

"I got a B and four stars, mum."

After Natalie had hung up her coat she flopped herself onto the sofa and gazed across the lounge.

"That's all very artistic, Alex, very good, well done."

"What is?" replied Alex in a very confused tone.

"That pattern on the table with all those old buttons and coins."

"I thought you did that, mum, that's why I left it."

Suddenly Natalie recoiled backwards as she knew what this was all about. "I think we had better pack this all away, don't you think, and let's get the dinner on the go."

Alex could see that his mother was shocked and upset about something, but after the two of them had finished their evening meal, Natalie suggested that the two of them should share the sofa bed and prayed that they would have a good night's sleep. Since Steve's death the two of them had made a very special bond between themselves and found that sleeping on the sofa bed had certainly helped put the grief of the past behind them.

It was about 1.30 am that Natalie awoke to feel a young tender hand feeling and caressing her arm and fingers.

"OK, Alex, that's enough," she moaned in her sleep.

Thirty seconds later it held her hand and began to give counting motions on the bones in her hand.

"Stop it, Alex!"

It started again until she opened her eyes and to her dismay a young girl of about five years old with a faint innocent smile and long blonde hair wearing a long Victorian dress stood by her pillow. Her aristocratic angelic face did not change expression but gave a very enigmatic stare into her eyes and then after a few shy seconds, the young child then raised her right hand, waved and skipped through the wall.

"Oh well, it looks as though I'll have to learn to live with a child ghost," sighed Natalie in a very tired but forgiving tone. "At least its not that bloody black thing with the oversized nose." A strange sickly smell of lavender filled the room, which was not unusual when a ghost had made an appearance, then as she lay there a stream of thoughts came flowing into her mind. Her new job was to start in a week's time and with an optimistic view, she hoped for a new future and to meet those that would give her the support needed at a very downward time in her life. Gripping her son with a tender firm grip, she turned over and soon returned to sleep.

The following afternoon, the atmosphere in the bungalow took a very mysteriously serious tone. As usual Natalie arrived home late afternoon but unusually the home was empty for that time of day. Alex had already left a message on the answer phone saying that he was spending a couple of hours at his friend's house and would be home by six o'clock.

"Good, no bills," exclaimed Natalie as she walked through the hallway and into the lounge, throwing her coat onto the sofa. Upon checking the lounge she noticed a piece of A4 sized paper on the dining room table with a short message in very childish copper plate writing. She knew this did not come from Alex, but the other clue sent an icy chill down her spine.

"Will you come and play with me later?"

"My God, what the hell do I do?" she thought, at the same time trying to stop herself from shaking and dropping the note. Suddenly she took a huge grip of herself and tore the page in four and threw it into the kitchen bin.

"To bloody hell with it all. I'll have to persuade her to go and see her mum and not me. I already have a son and the last thing I need is a lonely lost child trying to hitch itself onto me."

Later that evening the two of them finished their evening

meals and after Alex had completed his homework, both of them got ready for a warm relaxing evening in front of the television. Strangely enough the video of "Home Alone" had just been released about a young boy who had been accidentally left behind by his parents as they went abroad on winter vacation. As the News at Ten finished, Natalie began to dwell on a chance encounter with a tall, elegant looking man from the sales department at her new job. He was single and showed a lot of interest in her and with the Christmas party at a good quality hotel, she dwelled on having a nice evening in his company. Her new job was very demanding and made her feel totally drained by five o'clock but even so it was time to get to bed. Natalie's mind pondered on many issues. Alex was again without a father for the second time.

"Oh my God, what do I do now? Oh bloody hell!"

As she drifted off to sleep, the full moon soon began to be hidden by thick grim clouds until the whole sky went totally black. As she lay there, her whole bedroom became engulfed in total darkness while the digital clock at 11.22 pm gave the time from the far end of her bedroom. As she turned over she sensed a coldness at the sides of her legs. It seemed all to familiar as the juddering pulsating sensation moved around her bed and stopped.

"In the blood of Jesus I command you to go!" she snapped in an angry tone. That moment she felt at peace with herself as a feeling of warmth filled her mind. As she drifted into a deep slumber the silence of her home felt like a sense of empty vacuum so empty that a presence had to fill it by its own command.

"Stop that! Stop that now!" spat Natalie as she knew that her young friend had returned. As she opened her eyes the figure of the young girl was again beside her pillow.

"Go and see your mother, now!" ordered Natalie, digging her heels in with an uncompromising tone.

As she sat up in bed she stared at the child with her severe eastern European expression. The girl lowered her head then quickly turned around and ran through the wall behind her as though she was returning to a beloved parent.

"She's gone, let's hope she's got the message and stays gone."

As she returned to her weary slumber, she had a suspicious feeling that she had not heard the last of that night's encounter.

The following morning at the office, the Post Room girl was busy standing on her swivel chair putting up the Christmas tree decorations.

"Are you ready for the Christmas party, Natalie?"

"No, not really, Rachel. I need to get the time to buy some new clothes but I've been all around but I can't find anything that suits me at all."

"You should try Debenhams in Staines, they've got a thirty percent sale on Friday and Saturday. You should give them a go, much better than Marks."

"Oh, thanks for your advice."

Suddenly Rachel's eyes lifted to a figure that was standing beside her. It was Aaron the sales deputy, who had found an excuse to come over for a chat.

"How's life with you, Aaron?"

He grinned slightly as his eyes opened in wide circles like newly tendered coins from the Royal Mint.

"Oh, can't grumble, went to see that new Bond film with Catherine last night, the film was fine but we're not really hitting it off to be honest. Since the last guy she went out with, she finds it hard to trust blokes. You know it's the old matter of personalities and chemistry."

Natalie admired his honesty as it proved he was a genuine normal chap and not the type too desperate for a lady. His attractive blond complexion showed he had a lot of promise, very similar to Steve's, which, if given a clear chance, she would be only too keen to take up.

"The party." said Rachel in an almost abrupt voice.

"Oh that, I might come as it depends if I can get back from Paris on time."

Judging by his reply, it seemed that Aaron was playing hard to get, but Natalie knew enough about men to know what was really going through his mind.

"Anyway, you know that new application for M and M Services, well their credit account is enough for five thousand each month for thirty days, so if you'd like to set up a database today then that should action their new account."

"Not a problem," Natalie replied.

The two of them smiled at each other for several moments while the body language said the rest.

That evening, Natalie arrived home with her head buzzing with all sorts of new ideas. The first one was the managers she had met at the office, and also her home which she had decided to put up for sale so they could start a new life.

"What's that you're doing, mum?" asked Alex as she quickly searched the property section of the *Aldershot News*.

"Oh, I'm just looking for a new and better home closer to my new place of work."

"You mean, you're thinking of moving?"

"Well, yes, possibly. We've been here a year and I think we need a new change for the better."

She put an affectionate arm around him as he came to sit beside her on the sofa.

"You see, I've recently met this nice new man and he would like us to meet up just before Christmas and possibly move to Woking."

"Oh I see, I was hoping it would be just you and me for a while, mum. I still miss Steve and I want him back."

"Yes, I know, dear, but we've got to move on."

His attention then moved onto the Comet and Curry's advertisements for PlayStations and X-boxes.

"Look, mum, only one hundred and fifty pounds."

Natalie's eyes opened wide and then rolled upwards.

"My God, where am I going to get that money from, when I need new clothes for Christmas?"

The euphoria of December was certainly taking them both on an unknown journey. As both of them got into bed that night, Natalie totally forgot what was lurking in the background and was awoken in the early hours by an old woman holding the hand of the young girl.

"Oh hell, what is it this time!"

The woman looked angry but the young girl did not come forward to take Natalie's hand.

Instead they lowered their heads and the woman crossed her arms and shook her head before they both turned around and disappeared towards the hallway.

"That does it, I'm going to put this bloody place up for sale and start a fresh new year."

After dozing for fifteen minutes she was re-awoken by a new presence of the black angelic being standing right beside her pillow. She looked up at its severe persona with its white slits for eyes and its arms folded.

"You again, what's the matter with you? Aren't you fed up standing by doorways?"

It then hastily turned sideways and then slid through the wall as though is was gliding on a cushion of air.

"That's right, mate, you clear off," she muttered as it vacated the space next to her bed.

"Aarrgghh!" The following morning Natalie woke with a shock as if her mind had reached the climax of a bad dream.

"Clothes," that was the order of the day as she peeped through the gap in the curtains and surveyed the frosty black panorama outside her window.

"Well, let's hope my shopping adventures of today show better promise than the weather."

The good thing about that morning was that Alex had just received a telephone call that his new friend Matt had wanted to come round and keep him company, thus leaving her free to scan all the shops in Staines High Street.

"What a perfect situation, a woman left alone to her own devices. You don't get that very often. Now, what shops are there to see, Army and Navy, Debenhams, Alders, Top Shop. I've just got to get the right outfit at the right price to get this man's attention for next Saturday night."

The whole of the Elmsleigh Centre was crawling with activity that morning until she finally chose a black satin evening dress by Christian Dior. Natalie was a very lucky woman when it came to choosing clothes as she had a slender figure of perfect proportion. Many of the other girls always felt jealous of her as they all knew that for every occasion she was outstandingly attractive with her natural Ukrainian beauty.

"What was the meaning of the angelic being last night? Was this a meaning or threat of some kind? Am I in danger?" A cold tingle ran all the way down her back as she slightly shuddered. The thoughts of Steve still glided across her heart as she still missed the man in her life. Perhaps she was running into things too quickly and wanted to expect too much too soon. As the train eventually came to a slow gliding stop half a mile from her bungalow, she began to get feelings and visions that her destiny was already being planned by a sense from another dimension that had been pursuing her for the best part of a year. As soon as she put the kettle on the boil for a six o'clock cup of tea, the telephone rang from across the road. It was Lena, the lady she had met by accident in the queue at the local Post Office.

"Natalie, last night I had the most alarming dream. I saw

you shaking hands with other men and holding a tall man with blond hair amongst a crowd of people and you and this other man had a fog of evil all around you like a glow of awful grey."

"Oh, I see," said Natalie in a rather negative, "I don't want to hear any more bad news" voice. Lena was a very pessimistic person that revelled in bad news and Natalie was trying to rebel against such barriers that were trying to hold her back.

That evening the atmosphere at home was one of very stony silence.

"Huh, why should I let these people make my life so dull and boring? I'd like a man to inject some zest into my life again and take me out to that Russian club in the West End for a twist and shout."

As she sat there painting her fingernails with a rather expensive product she had bought from Beauty Base, Alex had returned home with a cheap disposable Kodak camera and began to nag his mother into taking her photo for the last photo shot so that he could get the film developed with him and his friends at the school disco held last week.

"Oh go on, mum, just one."

"Alex, make it quick as I'm in no mood to play your stupid games."

Her attitude towards her son could be a bit negative at times as it was her ex-husband's choice to have a child so soon after they got married.

Click went the camera as the cheap plastic mechanism gave its last shot.

"Done," said Alex as he stood up from his kneeling position. His mother pulled a very sarcastic face with her eyes.

"I'm off to bed in a moment as soon as my nails are dry. Have you done your homework yet?"

"Ummm, yes."

"I hear a certain amount of doubt there, my boy. I'd better start checking your books again, I'm not entirely convinced you're playing the game."

The following afternoon Alex arrived home from school in a very mixed mood. He had received a dreadful grade for his science homework with a red aggressive circle around it with a copper plate E in the middle of it.

"And what news have you got today, Alex? How did that awful physics homework go, the one you spent three days trying to do?"

"Oh, I got a B –" but his mother could see by his doubting face that he was not telling the truth.

"Alex, bring me your book, I want to see what's going on."

As she flicked through the pages to the end contents, she broke the silence with an aggressive serious tone.

"E …E. How low do you go, boy? Get out of my sight!"

After barricading himself in his bedroom for an hour, he finally came out holding a thick yellow envelope with the photographs that had been taken a week before.

"There's me and Matt and two others from my class."

"These girls look as though they are wearing too much make up for my liking."

Eventually Alex came to the end photo of his mother.

"Oh, this one looks a bit peculiar," as the two of them frowned with total bewilderment.

To Natalie's left arm was the figure of a young Victorian girl trying to get her attention as her face seemed distressed and tearful.

"My God," whispered Natalie in a very melodramatic tone as she knew who it was and snatched the photo from Alex's fingers.

"What's wrong, mum? Tell me who that is!"

"Oh, it's a reflection from the television, you know, optical illusion and all that."

Alex just sneered at his mother.

"And don't look at me like that!"

She hastily pushed the photos back into the envelope and sat back onto the sofa and began to chew her thumb nail in a nervous tentative manner.

"What now?" she thought, her arms and shoulders clearly twitching with shock. Alex stood by his mother's side looking very confused by her emotions.

"Perhaps I should take these to Lena," she thought . "No! No, better not," as she knew that she would get over-emotional and take everything far too far.

The following morning, the office was full of high spirits. Aaron came swiftly strutting up to Natalie's desk with two large boxes under both arms.

"Hi ya, well I'm overloaded from all these visits I've made from the happy hunting ground. Tell you what, can you do me a favour? Can you take these off me?"

"Are you sure, Aaron? Let's be fair to everyone."

"It's OK, it's all kosher, are you still ready for Saturday?"

As she paused for a second, a few doubtful warning signs sprang into her mind, then her weakness got the better of her.

"Yes of course, my dear, Lena will be bringing us."

"Oh, by the way, you and me will be on Klaus's table."

"Excellent," she thought as she knew that this table would be reserved for the higher staff and managers. "Huh, fame at last," she thought as she smiled before taking a sip of her lemon tea.

Knock, knock, knock!

"Oh God, who's that? Answer that for me, Alex."

"Mum, it's Lena from across the road."

"Oh right, come on in, Lena."

"Natalie, I've had one of my visions that within the next few weeks you are going to have a fatal accident. Listen to me, Natalie, all you have to do is sit tight for a month and don't travel for a month and certainly don't travel to any places you haven't been to before."

"How the hell can I do that, Lena? Look, it's Christmas and this is the only time of year I get to get out."

Lena just looked back at Natalie, her eyes full of defeat, rather like an accountant asking his boss for a wage rise.

"Well, all I can do is tell you all the warning signs," she replied in a very disappointed tone.

"It's time I locked up now. I'm sorry but it's ten past eleven and I'm totally drained."

Natalie stood transfixed for a few minutes wondering what the hell was happening to her life. Over the past week her friendship with Aaron had definitely escalated and nothing on earth would stop her from enjoying a good looking man's company who certainly showed clear signs of finding her irresistibly attractive in more ways than one.

"Anyway, Natalie, I am very concerned about you, especially as you have a boy to care for. He needs you more than anything else in the world, especially as Steve is no longer around."

Suddenly, Natalie recoiled backwards as this remark caused her emotions to snap.

"That's enough of that!" she shouted back in an over-charged, melodramatic voice.

"I think its time I went," she sighed.

"Yes, I think it is time you went, Lena," replied Natalie in a totally exasperated voice.

As she lay in bed that night, the room began to transmit a convulsing, pulsating, juddering sensation which reminded her of the H G Wells film "The Time Machine". Her body became ice cold as sweat dripped from every pore in her body. The young ghostly girl did not show as it certainly seemed that all was united against her. Too nervous to open her mouth and speak, she thought to herself.

"OK, I won't go, I'll stay put for a while until this whole entity loses interest in me and moves on."

Her mind went to rest and her whole body felt warm and at peace again. The only thing that would not leave her obstinate mood was that she had already committed herself to Aaron, who had reserved her a seat on the directors' table. She realized there was no way out as if she did not accept this privilege then it would show a rejection of their company.

Chapter 15

"I'm telling you, Natalie, you should call him and say you're ill or something, these visions keep getting stronger and stronger," persisted Lena.

"I can't, you stupid cow. I need my job and what's more if I play my cards right I could get promotion and the wage rise that I really need. This my big chance, I've got to bloody go."

"On your head be it," snapped Lena as they both slammed down their telephones in arrogant defiance of each other. Natalie looked up at her wall clock which read 5.37 pm for Saturday 18 December.

"Come on, Natalie, look on the bright side of life. You've got a fabulous new evening dress and accessories for the occasion and a very good looking guy to take care of you for the evening. Let's go for it."

By seven o'clock she was ready. She had spent fifty minutes in the bath and used every expensive available hair product and pampering lotion to enhance her radiant beauty.

"There is no doubt about it, you're a stunning woman and you know it," she whispered to herself and pursed her lips to apply the final touches of lip colour.

"What time will you be home, mum?" asked Alex as he leaned against the hot radiator with his hands in his pockets. Natalie could see he was not happy that she was spending the evening with another man that he had not met before.

"Don't worry, Alex, Julia will be here to keep you company for the whole of the night. She'll be here any moment."

"Mum, you don't have to go."

"Alex, look," she bent down to look him in the eyes.

"even mums and dads have to have some fun and enjoyment sometimes. There's more to life than going to work and washing and ironing."

"Yes, OK, mum, but please come home when you're finished."

"I will be home later, now don't worry."

Five minutes later the doorbell rang with its usual Westminster chimes.

"Ah, that must be Julia now," as she strutted up the hall way to offer her usual welcome routine to an old family friend.

"Oh hi, come on in … and Aaron, what a pleasant surprise."

"Hi Natalie, by chance we met outside as Aaron here was trying to find what number you lived at in the dark." She beamed as Aaron looked obviously impressed with his date for the evening.

"Can you just give me a few minutes as I need to speak to Julia to tell her what she has to do for the evening."

"Now, in case of emergency you can call me on this mobile number. I'll call you about ten or ten thirty to tell you what time I will be home." She then kissed her and Alex good night and then focused her attention on Aaron, who stood in the hallway checking his appearance in the wall mirror.

"OK, are you ready? Let's go." Taking her by the hand, he led her out to the Mercedes Compressor that he had meticulously cleaned that day. Instead of the usual talk of shopping and the moans and groans of paying bills, Aaron spoke about his early days growing up in Australia outside Melbourne and the typical boyish pranks and larking about that he did with his friends. His accent highly amused her and before she knew it, both of them were on a romantic high that was a launch pad for the most perfect endearing occasion.

"Aaron … were you ever married before?"

"Yes, about five years ago, but we found the strain of being together just got too much and she wanted a divorce which came as a bolt out of he blue."

"Oh I see," replied Natalie, relieved that he was being honest about his past. "I had a previous experience about twelve years ago but that can be just married life. Life goes on but you always learn from the experience."

"Gawd strewth, watch it ya daft dingo!" As he went for the brakes, she erupted into a bawl of laughter realizing that she had met the man that would make her life a new and righteous one.

Twenty minutes later, the car pulled into the hotel car park, its bright ornate lighting displaying the full lucrative splendour of the evening they were to about to enjoy.

"Strewth, this place looks a bit on the up-market side. Let's hope the tuckers alright, I'm feeling a bit peckish, let's go inside."

The two of them felt at ease with each other as they both came from a social background where Jack was as good as his master.

"I was in two minds about coming out tonight but this is turning out to be the best evening I've had in years."

Aaron just kept a straight face as his attention was drawn to the large oak reception desk to his left.

"Can you tell us where the Winchester suite is, please?"

"Second floor on the left," replied the brunette girl in her official uniform with name brooch.

"No worries," he replied as his face looked as though he couldn't make up his mind which lady he felt attracted to. As the two of them gracefully strolled into the immaculately laden executive suite, they were very warmly greeted by some very familiar faces from the senior management, in fact more attention was drawn to Natalie than Aaron. She noticed that their handshakes were far different from the usual welders' mitts she had encountered from previous companies. Trays of champagne were passed around as the directors were very keen to learn of Natalie's background and what she wanted to do with her future, which came as a refreshing experience for her as something she didn't get from her previous job.

"Do you feel that you would consider a moving to sales? Have you done quotations?" All these questions were put to her as she was only to keen to give a positive reply without sounding too naïve and vulnerable. Aaron became deeply involved in an intense discussion with Natalie's boss, which distracted him from the attention being given by the other ladies, then by 7.45 a gong was sounded to announce that all should be seating for serving. Aaron pulled out Natalie's chair and at last they were together again. Between the two of them, they stimulated the whole table with their life stories as they gave testimony of times of euphoria and times just too sad. They had clearly stolen the show as no other manager could contribute such worldly scenarios of joy, tears and gladness never heard of before. As the porter lit the gas lamps on the patio outside, they all began to adjourn to the terrace for fresh air and liqueurs.

"Well, we don't want to put their noses out of joint so we had better go with the flow."

"You'd better lead the way, Aaron, but keep away from all that smelly old cigar smoke. You know I can't bear it."

"I'm glad I gave it up when I did, which reminds me, are you alright for a refill?" enquired Aaron as he pulled on his velvet burgundy evening jacket. As the two went arm and arm, they realized they had only themselves.

"It seems ridiculous, Aaron, but I was advised to stay at home tonight to avoid to avoid a terrible misfortune. What has actually happened has turned out to be the most charismatic time in years."

He smiled with sympathy that he shared mutual feelings for her.

"Well, when I got the invite to the management night, I knew that I had to give it a lash." Suddenly his face turned with a serious expression followed by an abrupt question. "Are you here for good?"

"Sorry, what do you mean?"

"Well, you're not from England, right?"

"Well … um … yes, I have my marriage visa but I am no longer with my husband, he was killed not so long ago in a car incident that is still being investigated by the police."

"Phaw, strewth, poor blighter. I knew of a similar incident years ago in the northern territories where all the bums hang out."

The two of them became aware that they had hit a low point in their conversation and then looked into each other's eyes.

"Well, Natalie, I hope you've got a glass to gargle cos here's to a happy new year."

"Of course, we always celebrate new year more than Christmas in Ukraine."

"Yeah, too right, same shit, different year."

Aaron then burst into a roar of Aussie (this word does not exist and I don't know what you meant) laughter which Natalie was not at all amused with, as she was aware that the foul language was caused by consumption of lager and after dinner liqueur, something she had good experience with when socializing with men from her own native country.

"Are you sure you're alright to drive, Aaron?"

"What!? Yeah, course I'm alright. It's only half an hour from 'ere, we'll be OK."

Just at that moment, the barman called out last orders and struck his gong.

"Well, I'll have one for the road. Care for another?"

"No! And neither should you. You've had more than enough."

Aaron stood there rooted to the ground, his shoulders swaying slightly and his eyes as round as organ stops with the sides of his mouth pointing downwards. He had underestimated Natalie's disapproving firm streak and surrendered himself to her better judgement. It was now approaching midnight and she had forgotten the advise given by Lena.

"I think its time we hit the road, Natalie, I'll just pass the word around that we're offski."

As he disappeared into the hotel, Natalie scurried off to the reception desk to book a taxi. As the suited woman tried several numbers she lifted her face and broke some very negative news: "not for another two hours."

"Oh bloody hell no, I'm stuck with a pickled Aussie that must be unfit to drive!"

Suddenly there was a hand around her waist and she turned around.

"All set?" came the slightly slurred voice of her evening companion.

There was a moment's silence as Aaron stood totally cool, calm and collected with a devil may dare look on his face.

"Yes, certainly, let's go," she replied with a nervous tone of sheer surrender.

To Natalie's astonishment, Aaron seemed rather composed as though he was in control of himself, as though a great load had been taken off his mind.

"Oh just let him be himself, after all it is Christmas," as he put his arm around her waist and led her out to the car park.

"Are you sure you're OK to drive as we can get a taxi or another lift?"

"Of course I can," he replied in a very charming sing-song tone, at the same time searching for his keys in all the pockets of his trouser and blazer.

Beep went the sound of the central locking as this was the starting signal that the journey

home was about to begin. As both of them slipped into the Mercedes Compressor, it became clear that Natalie had become the prisoner and Aaron was the jailer with the keys. With one turn of the ignition, the car burst into life, grinning like the cat that had the cream, the power assisted steering did a right turn and onto the A336 towards Camberley.

"You know the story about the kids in the buzz boats got a load of laughs," suggested Natalie.

"Yeah, well, that's one of my old favourites, or the one about Ashley Garratt, the school swot that was after every prize at the end of term and all he got was booing from the audience. If you can make people laugh then you're gonna be popular."

"You make me laugh, you vulgar hound."

"Woof, woof," he replied as he found it hard to concentrate on the road, at the same time glancing at Natalie's beautiful night complexion as the passing of street lamps made repetitive long shadows on her side of the passenger seat.

"Oh look, it's starting to sleet."

"That's the thing about English weather, we don't get anything like this down under."

"Aaron, look, the roads are getting narrow, please slow down."

"Just relax, everything will be fine."

"By the way, what do you think of that stupid old fart Dave Saunders?"

"Oh, I think he's very sweet and friendly, he tells me that his eldest son has just finished University and is looking for a job in IT."

"Huh, no doubt he'll help his own flesh and blood find a good place in one of his mate's companies. It's not what you know, it's who you know. Right!"

"Right!" Natalie replied, to keep Aaron satisfied with his biased judgement.

"That's funny, I thought this was the way back to Lightwater," moaned Aaron, screwing his face up.

"Just keep going, Aaron, we'll come to some signposts sooner or later."

"Well I hope it'll be sooner cos I've got a creepy feeling I'm going the wrong way."

"Look, turn the car around, Aaron, and just go back, that's the safest way."

"OK, OK, but we'll have to find a roundabout or something. Ah good, Camberley five miles," he cheered as a lonely familiar road sign caught his head lights.

"Aaron, please slow down, you're doing almost sixty in a forty limit!"

"Relax, honey, there are no coppers round this neck of the woods, they're probably concentrating on those clubs and drug dens over at Aldershot."

"Alright, just keep your eyes on the road and make sure we get home soon."

"Ah, sounds like the offer of an invite in for a nice black coffee."

"I wouldn't invite you in to my home if you were the last man on earth, you're half drunk!"

"It's all the same with you Sheilas, always playing it hard to get."

He turned his head, roaring with laughter, to see what Natalie's facial expression was, only to see in the darkness that her lips were tightly sealed together with thick dark red lipstick, causing a critical lapse of concentration.

"Stop! Stop!"

"Aaaarrrhhhh shit!" went cries of raw shock as Aaron's right foot went for the brake pedal.

Screeeeech! There was a flash of red traffic lights and tail brake lights of a freight box truck that had come to a halt in front.

"Holy Cow!" *Screeeeeeech -Baaannngggggg!* as Aaron's Mercedes hit the tail end of the curtain side lorry with total precision accuracy. Both he and Natalie were thrown forward with the car in fifth gear, Aaron's airbag went into action cushioning the heavy velocity impact between his chest and the steering wheel. Natalie's failed to eject as she was throw backwards in a circus ring whip lash motion.

"Holy crap," groaned Aaron. There was a deathly silence for about fifteen seconds in total darkness until the next words were spoken.

"Are you alright, Natalie? Speak to me, Natalie!"

After a long pause a croaky voice came from his left hand side.

"I'm OK but only just, my neck and back are all stiff bit I think I've no broken bones."

"Well, thank Christ for that," he replied in a relieved Aussie slur.

Tap, tap, tap came a knock from Aaron's driver's window as a man wearing driver's overalls stood with his face hard against the glass.

"You alright, mate?"

"Yeah, I think we are, now comes the hard bit."

As he crawled out of the car, all that could be heard was the hissing of leaking steam from the punctured mangled radiator and the smell of leaking anti-freeze.

"Fucking hell, the car looks a write off to me," gasped the driver as he scratched the back of his shaven head.

"Hah, you really know how to cheer somebody up," growled Aaron at the driver with his two days stubble on his face.

"Look, mate, it's all your fault so don't blame me!"

"No one's blaming you!"

"Well, my truck's got it's tail plate all smashed in but I think that's about all. The lights didn't catch any of the blow due to the width of my back end. Are you with the AA or something that can help?"

"Yeah, course," he snapped in a totally gutted tone.

"Is the lady OK or should we get her to hospital?"

"Just a minute, I'll go and ask."

"Do you think you need to go to hospital, Natalie?" enquired Aaron, clearly hoping that he could be relieved from this laborious task.

"I'm pretty sure I'll be fine but could you please get me home because Alex and Julia are waiting for me."

"She's OK, but I need to make a call to the AA."

Five minutes later the call was made to get the vehicle towed to he nearest repair garage, during which time the driver wandered off to his cab to retrieve his pen and accident report forms . "Well, I'm going to have to put you down as the guilty party," proclaimed the driver in a no nonsense tone. "I'll wait until your chap turns up in case you need any help."

Aaron didn't reply as she stared in total disbelief at the crushed front end of his car. What was worse was that he had only been with his employer less than six months. "Bloody hell," he groaned.

Forty minutes later, there appeared in the dark distance a pair of sharp, bright headlights as a luminous yellow recovery truck appeared with its flashing lights on its roof.

"Right, take off the hand brake and I'll do the rest," as the winching gear went into action, as both of them slowly and tentatively climbed into the passenger side of the cab, Natalie being assisted with her whiplash injury. It seemed a chronic way of ending the evening, starting out being chauffer driven in a Mercedes to a very up-market dinner party and then ending the night having a detrimental car cash and being transported back home in a breakdown truck. How romantic!

The two of them just sat there all dressed in evening wear as the driver started up his engine with his top button undone and his chest hair exposed.

"Could you take the lady home first, buddy, she lives off the Watchmoor Park roundabout, Junction fifteen."

"Oh yeah, I know," nodded the driver as he adjusted the blower on his dashboard.

All three of them just sat there staring at the road in front in total silence, until they finally reached the driveway outside Natalie's bungalow.

"Aaron, can you help me down, I suddenly feel so dizzy and sick."

As they finally made it to her front door, Julia opened it in total disbelief at what she saw.

"My God! What happened?" as she saw the damage to Aaron's car under the light from the street lamp.

"Don't ask, Julia. I've had a nightmare of an evening."

Aaron breathed out heavily, making a raspberry rasping noise with his lips as he overheard Natalie's reply.

"I've got to have a lie down, I think I feel I'm going to faint I feel so sick."

"My God, you look as white as ghost. I'd better call a doctor or an ambulance!" Aaron then chimed in with a remark that would be the final icing on the cake. "Look, love, I think there's no need for all that, these Sheilas wear a lot of all this heavy make up which makes them look pale and ghastly."

"You stupid idiot! Don't you think you've made enough trouble for one evening?" yelled Julia as she put a cold face flannel under the kitchen tap.

"What's the matter, mum?" whinged Alex as he appeared at the lounge door.

"Your mum has had a very funny turn but I think she'll be OK. Go and lie on the bed and I'll call the doctor. Do you know the telephone number, Alex?"

"Eh, do you think you still need me? The AA man is still outside." There was a moment's silence as Julia contemplated what was more important.

"Yes, I think that's all you can do," Julia replied.

"OK, I might ring tomorrow to see if she's alright. I think she should take Monday off work to recover from the shock. I'll be off then, goodnight all."

Aaron then gave a brief wave with his left hand and let himself out. Julia then turned her attention to the telephone book and searched under "D" with her quivering fingers.

"I think his name is Latimer," said Alex as he leaned against the banisters.

"Ah, here it is, now go and check that your mum is alright. Hello, this is Julia Tokareva calling from Harley Meadows. I need a doctor to call here as soon as possible as my friend Natalie Harrison has returned home following a car accident."

"Well, the next available doctor will be with you in about an hour," replied the emergency telephonist.

"Can anybody come any sooner? … Then we'll have to just sit tight until somebody eventually comes."

As soon as she put the receiver down, she rushed into the bedroom where Natalie lay all hunched over, her face as white as a Marcel Marceau impressionist.

"I'm doing alright, Julia, how long do I have to wait?"

"My God, you're all ice cold. The doctor will be about fifty minutes."

Natalie did not look up at Julia at all. She just stared, her eyes transfixed on the framed photograph of her late husband, Steve, standing on the bedside cabinet.

"I did love him, Julia, in fact I was absolutely captivated with him from the start." Her mind flashed back five years to when they both stood in a long queue outside the British embassy in six inches of snow.

"We did everything we could for each other. Two weeks

128

after we met he returned to England promising that he would return with all the documents for me to come to England and get married. Four months later he kept his promise and we met again at Kiev airport. Of all those that were refused their UK visas, I was given mine without the interview. Don't you see, we were meant to be together as husband and wife. We really loved each other." Her voice just faded away into a whisper as Julia replied in a pull yourself together tone.

"I'll call again and see what's happened to the doctor."

"Another fifteen minutes, Natalie. … Natalie?" There was no answer as she lay there with her back to her and her head totally resting on the pillow.

"Natalie, wake up, he'll be here quite soon." Alex came tearing into the room, aware of the situation, and shook his mother frantically by the shoulder.

"Mum! Mum! Wake up! Speak to me!"

There was absolutely no response or sign of life, as her blue grey eyes did not even blink or move as they still stayed focused on her late husband's bedside photograph.

"She's dead," whispered Julia in a tone that was so profoundly sad it could have moved the most hardened of hearts. There was a breeze of sheer ice cold that swept the whole room as they both got off the bed and gazed at the boy's mother.

"Alex, let's go next door and wait for the doctor."

"It's too late, auntie Julia, my mum's dead, nothing can ever bring her back."

There weren't any tears from both of them as they sat hand in hand on the sofa staring at the Christmas cards until finally an abrupt chime from the doorbell alerted them that the doctor had arrived. "Oh good evening, I hear that a young lady has been involved in a car accident tonight," as the short stocky man in his early forties stepped in wearing a zip up utility anorak. He wasn't given a formal greeting, but he could tell by

129

the expression on their faces that the situation spoke for itself.

"She's in this bedroom and we know she's been dead about twenty minutes," spoke Julia in a cold melodramatic voice. The doctor didn't reply, he just turned his head and shuffled his way into the room and lifted Natalie's right hand to feel her pulse. He felt nothing. He then clipped his stethoscope into his ears and unfastened the front of her black satin evening dress and checked her heart beat. Again, there was nothing. As Julia and Alex stood just inside the doorway, they saw the man's face wince. It seemed that the news that he had to give them was more difficult than the death of the woman that was lying in front of them. He paused for several moments and looked Julia right in the eye.

"Yes, I'm afraid you're right. Normally these symptoms of death are usually caused by a ruptured aorta. Very tragic . How old was she?"

"Thirty four," replied Julia.

The doctor gritted his teeth and explained that he had to get the body removed to the nearest hospital for the postmortem.

"As Frimley Park hospital is the nearest I shall contact them myself. Can I use your telephone?"

Alex stood alone in the sheer quietness of the room staring at his mother's face. He kept thinking to himself, "She's not dead, she'll wake up any minute now," but she never did.

Fifteen minutes later the doctor had written out all the necessary documents. Suddenly Julia appeared and led him away to the lounge.

"Alex, look into my eyes, you've got to be strong. Your mother was a wonderful woman. Always remember that you had the best mum that any son could wish for. Why this happened tonight you and I will never know the answer."

Alex's face tightened into contorted anger. "I know why she died! They killed her!"

"Who?"

"Them, those bloody bastard ghosts that killed Steve!"

"I've got to inform your mum's family in the Ukraine, now where are all the necessary telephone numbers? Now in the meantime I think you should come and stay with me until I get instructions. It could be possible that you are to return home."

"Sounds like a great idea cos all my friends are at home. I never made any friends here cos I'm foreign."

"I know it's a very difficult situation in this country, Alex, but you're not the only one. I get it as well. There are those at my office that won't include me in their conversations so I know when I'm not wanted. What will most probably happen is that you'll return to the Ukraine as there are no blood relatives here in England." Julia briefly searched the bungalow, then suddenly the doorbell rang.

The doctor intervened, "I'll deal with all this, Julia," then two ambulance men arrived with a stocky lady all dressed up in hospital uniforms with a mobile stretcher to remove the body. It seemed all most unlikely that this scenario could be kept a secret from the neighbours as by now all of them were peering through their curtains to see what all the commotion was all about.

Chapter 16

That night Alex fought with his inner emotions. His mother was now dead and he lay there in total fear of his own life as both his parents had been killed within the past twelve months. Would he be next? By half past four he slipped away into a shallow doze as memories of his childhood flicked through his mind.

"Huh? What, huh?" he stuttered as Julia shook his shoulder.

"Alex, I've made you some breakfast. It's already quarter past seven." He just lay there, his eyes staring at the ceiling as he realized that yesterday was not just a nightmare but actual reality.

"I've spoken to your father in Mogiliv – Podilsky and he's totally shocked about what has happened. He could not say too much but he insisted that you must return to the Ukraine within the next month. I'll be looking after you until then, if you need anything from the flat then come and ask me and I will go and get it."

"Thanks a lot, auntie Julia, but I still have my front door key."

She frowned at him as it was bad luck to browse over a place of a close relative's death.

"I've left my football stuff behind in my bedroom."

"Clean or dirty?" replied Julia.

"Very muddy from yesterday morning's match, but that's what I need to get," replied Alex in a very guilty tone.

"I'll go and get it now, it's in the dirty clothes box in the corner where we've always kept it."

"No, Alex, you stay here and wash the dishes and hoover the hallway carpet."

"You really know how to cheer a young bloke up, bloody woman," groaned Alex as she hastily slipped on her boots and slammed the door shut behind her.

As Julia approached the bungalow she stopped dead in her tracks. From the pavement outside the lounge window, she could see a dull amber light from behind the curtains that were still left closed from the previous night. As she approached the doorway with great caution, she clearly saw that some activity was going on inside, while she tried to unlock the front door with its stiff mechanism making a quiet screeching noise. As soon as she entered the hallway her body hair stood on end with the deathly cold atmosphere still stiff in the air. As she slowly peeped around the doorway of the living room she saw a figure of a man wearing a heavy jacket. After a few seconds, she could see that it was the ghost of Steven. Around him was a dark yellow glow of light. As Julia stood there, he gradually turned and made an acknowledgement with his head.

"You must look to the light. Look to the light and go in peace."

As he turned his head away, he looked in an upwards direction for several seconds and then slowly disappeared. The acoustics of the room changed and then there was a distinctive click sound.

"He's gone, he's made it over to the other side," she said in a quiet whisper as she stood there staring at the small space where he stood. She then turned away, rummaged through the dirty clothes box and found Alex's filthy odorous football kit.

As soon as she returned home she told Alex in precise detail what had happened. Of course this inspired him to sneak into the flat against her wishes, but even so he pretended that he was not interested, but Julia was typically suspicious that he was up to something behind her back. Due to compassionate reasons he was allowed a week off school and so he began to plan a secret visit to the house. The autopsy of his mother's body proved that she had died from heart failure caused from a ruptured aorta, just as the doctor had given on the night of her death. The funeral had been planned for the following Monday and all the invitations and news were given out to all her friends and associates from eastern Europe. Alex still had his front door key and despite strict orders not to enter the bungalow, he awaited the most secretive discreet time he could sneak back undetected. Everybody else had gone to work that dull dreary Wednesday morning, which was ideal for him to accomplish his mission to satisfy his enquiring mind. His heart began to pound and his whole body went cold as he slipped on his zip up jacket and made his way down the road to make his last farewell to his UK home.

Once inside, he made his way to his bedroom to find that the door was already open. As he slowly crept into his old room he was hit by an almighty shock. On the bedroom wall was a message in black block capitals made by thick felt tip pen which said,

"Boy, you are not in any danger. We will not harm you. You are a naïve child. The only people that are in danger are those who seek to wage conflict with us. We were called here and have to stay here. If we leave then hell awaits us. Go now and tell others that we must be left to rest here. Others had to be killed as they decided to rid us of our place of rest."

Alex recoiled backwards until he hit the wall behind him. "I've got to get out of this place!" After gathering his energy and emotions, he left the bungalow, running like a greyhound after the rabbit at White City. "How do I tell Julia about this?"

"What's the matter?"

"Nothing, Julia."

"Pardon the pun but you look as though you've just seen a ghost."

"Well, as I went out to the shop this morning, I looked through my bedroom window at the bungalow and there was a message in black marker all over my bedroom wall."

"Really?" replied Julia in a very curious tone.

Alex explained in great detail as a typical youngster showed great interest in this paranormal experience.

"In that case you'd better show me." The two of them made their way to the bungalow and after unlocking the front door Alex began to tremble as he feared some rebellion from the unknown.

"Look, here it is."

"Where? I don't see anything."

"How can you say that, Julia? Look, I'll read it to you."

As Alex read it aloud, she became aware that something extraordinary was going on as she had seen the ghostly figure of Steve the day before. In the paranormal world it is possible for something to be seen by somebody and not by another person.

"As you know it will be your mother's funeral in about seven days' time, and I've got to make all the arrangements. Can you lend me your mother's address book so that I can contact those who would be interested in coming?"

Alex went over to the sideboard and pulled out a small red book full of all sorts of contacts, all neatly written in his mother's sharp eastern European handwriting.

Tap! Tap! Tap! Knock, knock, knock. "Ello, ello," came the noise at Julia's front door. It was Lena and she was in one of her terrible hyper-emotional moods.

"I told her about this and warned her that something fatal was going to happen," she said in a tone of absolute hysteria.

"I had a very clear dream the week before and told her to stay with Alex for the evening, but it's all too late now!"

There was a brief silence, then Julia tried to change the subject by adding, "Look, Lena, the funeral is in about seven days' time, Tuesday or Wednesday of next week, so the invitation is open to you so you're more than welcome to come."

"Oh, so that's the most you can say? My best friend is dead and I strongly feel, in fact I am totally convinced it's something to do with this place. Every time I went there my flesh began to crawl. Whatever is behind this, I'm determined to get to the bottom of it!"

Chapter 17

"OK, is everybody ready?" The black motorcade pulled up outside with a large Rolls Royce at the front. As everybody straightened their ties and jackets, they all squeezed into the back, most of them not looking up to look at the glossy oak coffin carefully displayed with wreaths in the back of the Mercedes Benz hearse.

It pulled away from the kerb in a totally silent fashion without the noise of a revving engine.

"Oh well, the weather has stayed good for the day, let's hope it all holds out," said Julia in a way that everyone should all cheer up and look forward to a good social do at the end.

"Is that all you can talk about, Julia, the bloody weather? The boy's parents have been killed within the last year and I know why. Do you think that this demonic force should be able to get away with it?"

Nobody answered.

"Well, if nobody won't do anything about it then we'll see about that."

Suddenly there was a quiet voice from the rear seat. It was Alex.

"If I were you I'd leave them alone. I've already had a message from them that they can't leave. You don't want to end up the same way as mum and dad, do you?"

Lena went very silent and stared at the traffic from her side of the window.

As the hearse pulled into the front drive of the church, the pall bearers disembarked and all stood to attention as a mark of conservative respect for the occasion. As the director in charge emerged from the front seat wearing his black top hat and tails he marched to the rear of the car, opened the door and, with the help of his staff, pulled out the coffin.

"There goes Natalie," groaned Julia, all dressed in black satin, as Lena stood behind her in a pose that said "you've not heard the last of this". She kept browsing at all the guests that had been invited, especially Alex, and after a few minutes made her way over to him to show some comfort and sympathy, even more so to get some information about what had happened over the last six months. With everyone doing a slow march they all entered the church vestibule and down the centre aisle, the atmosphere so quiet one could hear a mouse squeak. Most of those who came to attend were from the Russian church Ennismore Gardens in Knightsbridge and within half an hour had stood the length of the service, had sung the final hymn and followed the coffin out of the church to begin the journey to the cemetery.

"Alex, how would you like an evening out to Chinatown next week? I'm available next Thursday evening so if you like, Julia and myself can all go in my car and we can all have a nice evening out and enjoy," asked Lena, preparing him to surrender all the esoteric secrets that had occurred. He hesitated for a few moments as he stared at her thick lipstick on her canny smile.

"That sounds really good of you, Lena, but don't leave it too late as the food can get a bit old and chewy."

"It seems that you know more about this place than I do," she coyly replied. Lena was a shrewd crafty woman that knew that all boys loved restaurants, but most of all knew that Julia distrusted her and would not want to come, thus leaving Alex and her alone for the evening.

On the return journey after the funeral, all those invited were full of mixed emotions. It seemed totally unbelievable to discuss how both parents were killed in the most unfortunate bizarre circumstances.

"Well, Alex, how is your grandmother in the Ukraine?"

"She's fine but she's getting really old now."

"I remember the days when you and her used to share the same bed."

"Well, I won't be doing that anymore."

"Yes, you've certainly grown up a lot since you arrived in England."

"It's not just that, granny had the most awful wind and there's no way I'm going back to that.

I want my own bedroom just like the one I had here."

"Well, perhaps your father's new wife can fix you up."

As all the guests left the hall, they made a collection for Alex by putting twenty and fifty pound notes in a large biscuit tin covered in birthday wrapping paper that was situated by the dusty old piano.

"Don't worry, Alex, at least you won't be going home empty handed," said one elderly man with a long grey beard and a rather thick Polish accent. "Spend it wisely, lad, and don't blow it on a load of old rubbish."

"Oh, I won't. I want to buy a new computer that can do everything with internet and e-mail."

"Really," replied the man, "sounds good, whatever it is." Alex didn't explain what this all meant as he could tell that the elderly man's computer knowledge was very few and far between.

"Anyway, my boy, I must be off and I wish you all the very best of Polish luck … if there is any."

As the hall finally emptied, Lena reached out from behind Alex, put her right hand on his shoulder and clearly whispered, "See you at the end of your road at seven on Thursday." Alex lifted his head with interest as he hadn't been to a restaurant in months. They both knew that he would be there.

"What was Lena saying to you earlier, Alex?" enquired Julia. "Oh, she was just asking if I wanted a farewell party before I go back to the Ukraine."

"Well, whatever that woman says, just take it all with a pinch of salt. She's always been a nosey cow poking her nose into everybody's business, so don't suck up too closely to her. It's time you got ready for bed and make sure you clean your teeth well. All those cakes must have had God knows how much sugar in them."

As Alex lay in bed, a final thought came into his head. It was Tuesday night and he could easily say that he was going to his friend's house for supper, but Lena's words were engraved on his mind. "Be at the end of the road at seven." Lena was quite a good looking woman with a very good side and warm heart, somebody Alex could take all his troubles to and get it all off his chest. With all that had happened, he looked forward to his date with a very good appetite. As he lay there under the thick, soft, cotton duvet, his mind went over and over what he was going to do with himself for the next few days. His new friends had suggested that they all go to Coral Reef, a water world swimming pool with water chutes at Bracknell. He was in two minds about taking this up as the events of what had happened had left him physically and emotionally burned out, and without his mother he began to think who would taker her place. As his mind went around in circles, he turned over and started at the LED digital clock on the bedside table which had the same effect as counting sheep. Within fifteen minutes he was snoring like a pig.

Chapter 18

"Come on, Lena, where are you?" whispered Alex as he stood alone two feet from the kerb. It was five minutes past seven and she still hadn't made an appearance in her unwashed Peugeot that she had driven for the past year. He felt rather embarrassed as Alan, the elderly man that owned the bed and breakfast house opposite, began to give him very strange looks as though he was up to some kind of mischief.

Hoot, hoot came the noise of a small car horn as Lena finally arrived, pulling into the kerb and wearing a new black trouser suit from Next.

"Feeling hungry?" she asked with a most inviting smile on her face.

"You bet, let's go!" he replied.

As Alex jumped into the passenger seat all his fear and doubt disappeared as tonight he felt he was certainly with the right company.

"What sort of music are you into?" enquired Lena as she put her foot hard on the gas pedal to pull away sharply from the roadside.

"House and garage."

"What? Never heard of it, whatever it is –"

"Look out, you nearly hit that woman on the bike!"

"Oh never mind, Alex, just relax, its only ten minutes up the road."

As the two of them settled down at the table in the corner, the small Oriental waitress took their drinks order.

"I'll have a pineapple juice."

"Large or small?" she replied.

"Aw, large one please," and then Lena hesitated for a few seconds and then looked up from the wine list.

" A dry red wine." The waitress didn't reply as she just added the order to her list and finally added.

"Please help yourself to the soup or the buffet at the far end."

"Off you go, Alex, I'll just have the main meal."

After Lena had taken a long sip of her wine, she broke the silence with a very melodramatic tone. "How did all this happen?"

"What?" replied Alex, sounding somewhat confused.

"Don't you think that all this trouble that had happened has come from somewhere? I think you know what I'm talking about."

He looked up and was met with her seductive green eyes burning straight into his naïve blue pupils.

"What stood on that plot of land before Harley Meadows was built?" There was a very cold silence before he finally offered a reply.

"Well, I remember Steve getting a letter from the local council about a year ago. It explained that in the late sixties on the spot where our home is, a car mechanic's workshop was built and next to it was a doctor's surgery which was later used as a furniture showroom."

"And?" enquired Lena.

"Oh… I remember there was something mentioned about the garage, that there was some sort of club used to meet there for making contact with the spirit world and that they killed many animals in some kind of rituals and buried them at the back of the building. The whole gang were tipped off to the police and they were arrested and sent to prison. I think all this happened in the late sixties."

"Really? How extraordinary," whispered Lena. "Tell me more."

"I remember vaguely that when me and mum returned from the Ukraine, Steve was very worried and shocked about something as though he had had a nasty shock and didn't know what to do. That's all I can tell you."

"OK, that's enough," she calmly snapped but Alex could see that Lena was bothered by the whole scenario.

"What's up, Lena, you look really niffed about something."

By the time they had finished their dessert, Lena had gathered all the information she needed to hear and gave the final word for the evening.

"Look, I think its time we started getting back. It's almost eight thirty. Have you got everything?"

Ten minutes later, Alex was dropped off at the end of Julia's road but he was suspicious Lena was up to something.

"Well, I hope you enjoyed yourself, young man, keep in touch."

There was a slight hesitation in Alex's reply as he finally slammed the passenger door shut and made his way back to Julia's address. Suddenly he stopped dead in his tracks and looked back over his shoulder.

"I know where she's gone now, she's gone to snoop around our old bungalow," he whispered to himself. Alex then doubled back on himself and very quietly trotted to his old home, keeping very tight to the fences next to the pavement so as not to be seen by Lena if she were to check her driver's mirror to see if she was being followed. As the old garden wall came in sight he could see that her car was parked outside and she was about to go around the back to peer through the lounge window.

"Nosey cow," groaned Alex and within five minutes she had returned to the front gate and drove off looking confident as though she had not been spotted prowling around.

"Have a nice evening?" called Julia as Alex let himself in. "Alright, I suppose," he replied as though he was trying to convince her that he had met his usual friends for company.

"Come on, boy, where did you really go? And it wasn't to your mate's house. For a start you've left your bike here and I can smell spicy food on you."

"Alright, I've been out with somebody for dinner," he confessed after he realized that he was wasting his time denying it.

"And I know who, It's that nosey busybody Lena," snapped Julia.

"Yes it is," he snapped back.

"Well, I don't mind you being with her just as long as she doesn't try anything. I think you know what I mean."

"Don't be daft, she likes a man with loads of money. I haven't got two pennies to rub together."

As the two of them stood in the hallway gossiping about the evening, Lena was busy in her own garage, finding a blunt screwdriver or chisel so she could spring a latch to break into the bungalow at Harley Meadows.

"No, too sharp ... too narrow ... Ah, this one shows some good promise." As she stood there totally transfixed by the story that she had heard that evening, she became convinced that she would secure the defeat of the entities that had implemented the death of Steve and Natalie.

"Thy will be done," she whispered in the dark pungent smelling brick shelter situated at the back of her home.

"God, where is my crucifix? Ah I remember, ha ha ha ha ha." She sang a German folk tune as she swivelled around on her new stiletto heels and pointed in the direction of her bedroom, clicking her fingers and shrieking, "I have it!" She pulled open the storage drawer from under her double divan bed and pulled out an overnight case, which she had brought back from her last visit to her mother's.

As she rummaged around like a child looking for the free toy in a cereal packet, her fingers finally came across a large six inch brass orthodox cross which was by this time thick with tarnish.

"Blast it, when this was given to me it shone like a new penny, I'll have to go to Tesco to get some Brasso," she muttered to herself with disappointment. As she pulled on her overcoat and dashed out to her car, Lena had not thought through her motives. The forces that she had decided to challenge were of a kind totally unknown to her of which a victory for her certainly had no guarantee. The heavy crucifix lay on the soft cotton duvet. Would this duel culminate in a euphoric victory or would it be to her own detriment? Lena had overlooked one very important point. She hadn't any experience on how to perform an exorcism and she certainly had never heard of the armour of light. What she also didn't realize was that it would take more than a bronze cross to protect her from the spiritual defiance that still lay lurking at Harley Meadows. As she polished up her crucifix that night, her mind ran into an aggressive, egotistical mood. She pondered over the tough issues she had encountered in life and she felt so sure in her mind that she would succeed in defeating the entities that had driven the previous owners to their fate.

"Perfect!" exclaimed Lena as she held up the gleaming cross to the kitchen light. Suddenly at this point in time she became nervous as her mischievous smile dropped from the lower half of her face. She turned her head and looked out of the double glazed window into the pitch black darkness. The deafening eerie silence in her home spoke volumes as all she could feel was the pounding of her heart and the cold sweat pouring from her forehead. Looking up at the wall clock, her mind turned over the mission she was determined to carry out. It was 10.47 and the streets outside lay as quiet as those of

Buenos Aires during the military curfew some years before. Pulling on her dark grey overcoat, she slowly opened the front door and, grasping her bronze weapon inside her deep long pocket, she made her way out onto the pavement to begin the ten minute walk to Harley Meadows. Upon her arrival, she whispered some verses from the New Testament while surveying her best point of entry. The kitchen window at the back seemed the most practical as she could step over the kitchen surface once inside.

As she prised an old blunt chisel between the window sash and the frame, she persistently worked at the latch movement until the window eventually sprang open. Reaching inside, she opened the main window next to it and then stepped onto the kitchen unit.

"Come on, girl, pull yourself together," she uttered to herself as she slowly made her way to the door that led to the lounge. Everything so far seemed all very easy. Suddenly she remembered something. Her heavy cross still weighed deeply in her coat pocket and as she reached down deeply to pull it out, she became aware of an icy cold breeze coming from the far end of the hall.

"Harrgghh," breathed Lena as she pulled out the cross and firmly held it at arm's length at waist height. There was not a sound or a pin drop. As she stood there in a position that was rooted to the ground she gradually saw a black figure of an old woman wearing clothes of the Edwardian era. The two of them stood there about ten yards apart for fifteen seconds until the figure held up her right hand in a 'halt' position. As Lena's throat went totally dry, she stood her ground until the figure dropped its hand and bowed its head, turned and disappeared through the wall in a parade ground 'about turn' position.

"Phew, that was bloody scary," whispered Lena, "but what was it trying to tell me? It seemed very upset about something as though it was trying to warn me of some danger." With her cross held out in front of her she began to creep up the hallway until she came to the lounge doorway, which was left ajar. Pausing with anticipation, she stood still and breathing heavily. She felt that she about to enter a chamber that would threaten her life. Gripping her crucifix even more she raised her right foot and kicked open the panelled door. Pausing momentarily, she slowly stepped into the doorway until she arrived at the spot below the centre light. With her arm outstretched she turned around until she saw the clock on the far end wall. It clearly read 11.22. As she stood there staring at it, a shimmering cloud of smoke began to appear through the wall behind it as though somebody on the other side was pumping it through a pipe. Lena was totally traumatized as the smoke turned into a shimmering cloud that gave off a vapour like that seen at a petrol station.

"Oh hell, oh my God!" she screeched in a shrieking tone. The cloud came right at her with a swishing tail like that seen on a stingray. Desperately pointing her cross in its direction she felt an intense cold grip around her wrist, pressing all the more until she dropped the solid bronze object, which made a heavy clunking noise as it hit the floor.

"Who are you?" she screeched as the demon came to a slow stop above her head. There was no sound at all. Absolutely no answer.

"In the name of God I command you to go!"

As Lena looked up the demon began to fade and disappear.

"Thank God," she breathed as she felt that she was free from the icy grip until she heard the door slam behind her. Taking this chance to escape, she quickly knelt down and retrieved her crucifix and make a run for it, only to find that the door knob was stuck solid. As she fought frantically to open it, an old woman's voice in a London Cockney accent came from the other side, "Lena, Lena," and a small grey hand turned the knob on top of hers. Suddenly the door flew open, sending her tripping backwards on the floor. As she scrambled to her feet, she saw a flickering figure of an old woman giving directions with her hands to the kitchen where the back door was open.

"Go, girl, go!" she panted as she fled down the hallway and out into the back garden. Looking back over her shoulder she heard the door shut behind her.

"So round one to you, you satanic bastards. I'll return and take away the home you think you possess," she whispered as an evil chill wind blew through her hair as she buttoned up her coat and made her way back down the silent street to her humble abode.

Chapter 19

"Hello, hello, is that you, Julia?"

"Yes, it's me, Lena."

"I got your message you left last night on my answer phone. I'd like to say thank you for taking Alex out for the evening."

It was typical that a young boy had to let the cat out of the bag. Now Lena was in a very embarrassing and awkward situation as Julia was aware that she was up to something suspicious.

"Lena, if you have any ideas about Natalie's home you can just forget it. Look, girl, it's none of your business." For the next five minutes, Julia very wearily listened to her friend's opinions.

"How do you feel about the next family that will buy that home? They will get the same treatment that Steve and Natalie got. Don't you see that those horrible spirits have to go? They must be destroyed or they will kill again. You must understand this."

There was a stony silence for a few moments and then Julia replied, "On your head be it, girl, but you know the advice we were taught at school, always keep your nose clean and stay away from trouble. Give your brain a chance, Lena. Just drop the whole thing."

Then Julia put the receiver down with a very loud clunk.

"Mouthy cow," thought Lena as she sat on the arm of her sofa bed. Her mind was stuck between a rock and a hard place as she didn't know if she was coming or going with her emotions, especially the shock of seeing a dirty cloud demon coming through the wall and forcing her crucifix out of her hand.

"It seemed that there were good as well as bad spirits in that home as the ghost of the old lady forced open that jammed door and helped me to escape. Perhaps I should try and make a peace treaty with them and help them to leave and find a new place of rest. But how can I do this?" she whispered to herself as she filled up and switched on her electric kettle, as she leaned against the kitchen wall thinking it seemed that this was a stupid, dangerous task.

"No. They have got to go. Force must be met with force," she muttered to herself as she gazed out of her kitchen window into the night. Lena had been divorced for three years as she had met her husband in the Ukraine and got married on a six month fiancé visa. It all happened so quickly that they both got swept along with the romance of it all, but a year after they were married she put more and more pressure on him for a bigger and better material life. She longed for a detached house and her husband to be the breadwinner so that she could give up work and have a child. However, her soul mate had different ideas as he firmly believed that everyone should have job to go to and do it well. Since her divorce she had met and had several relationships with good potential partners as they all aspired to her Slavic volatile character, but there was the latest man that had captured her heart with his warm approachable personality. For the last two weeks he had been away on business in Argentina and upon his return, Lena was expecting him to propose. That following morning she was to receive a letter that would throw her life into a completely different perspective. As her mailbox made the usual clattering sound warning her of a postal arrival, she immediately recognized the pale blue air mail envelope with Darren's hand writing on it. She knew this was official news as she paused to regain her breath before opening it. The letter broke the news that he couldn't continue with their relationship, the reasons being that she was too dominant and strong willed and he was too laid back and easy going and the question of marriage would be a strained relationship. This didn't come as too much of a shock to her as she was aware that she had disturbed his easy going temperament.

"Oh well, that's another one gone to the wall," she sighed in resignation to defeat as she threw the screwed up paper ball into the kitchen bin. Her life had been full of many challenges, especially settling down in England, but there was one last challenge that still stuck in her mind, the death of her best friend, Natalie.

"If there is no way of forcing out the demons, then I'm going to take away their home," she hissed to herself as she ground her teeth before locking up and leaving for work. As a young girl, she was told about the Soviet scorched earth policy of dismantling all buildings so as to leave nothing of any use for the German invaders.

"Ah, that looks good," she muttered as she caught sight of an old petrol can on the upper shelf in her lock-up garage. As she picked it up by its grotty oily handle, it made a hollow sloshing noise, giving positive indication of its contents.

"Tonight ... No..." she mumbled to herself as she plotted her next move to defy the demonic power that stood its ground at Harley Meadows. After placing the container back on the shelf she got into her Volkswagen Golf (she had a Peugeot earlier) and reversed out of the garage. Little did she know that already time was ticking away for the duel that awaited her.

"Have you heard anything from Lena?" asked Julia to Alex as both of them started their evening meal.

"No, nothing at all," he replied with a deep frown on his bland adolescent face.

"It's quite usual for her to ring as she's always got a mouth as big as a garden shed. Perhaps I'll call her later to see what the latest gossip is."

Alex did not reply to this as he was suspicious that she was up to something of a subversive kind. "Did she tell you of any mad idea she had in mind, Alex?"

"Ummm … no, not that I can think of," he replied in a tone that sounded somewhat unsure.

Julia looked at him with an expression that doubted his words.

"You know, Alex, you should never play games with something that you don't know what you are playing with. It's as though you are lighting the fuse to a firework and you don't know the size of the explosion you are going to get. Do you know what I mean?"

"Yes, I'm pretty sure I do." It somewhat reminded of the demise of his family.

"Let's just hope that girl is not poking her nose into something that she'll live to regret," groaned Julia as she reached behind her to pick up the telephone receiver on the wall. After dialing the six digit number there was a pause for long moment until she got an answer.

"Hello, Lena, I haven't heard from you and, well, I thought that was strange. Is everything OK with you? OK, well, that's fine, I don't want to keep you long as you're just about to get into the bath. Yes, we're just checking that you're OK. What's that? You've split up with Darren? Oh, I'm sorry. Look, there's loads of men out there and a girl like you is in great demand so it'll be so easy to find a new man. I'm not being an interferer, I'm just doing my job as your friend, that's all."

As both women put their receivers down, Lena slipped off her dressing gown and very slowly lowered herself into the steaming hot bath until the water came up to her chest. There was a cold stillness in the air despite the hot mist that arose from the water.

"Huh," she gasped as she felt a two icy cold hands on each shoulder with a tingling caressing sensation. With calm composed movements she tried to move herself upwards, only to be met with a strong rigid grip that pushed her downwards until the water touched her chin.

"Yeeh!" she screamed as she reached out and desperately grabbed the radiator on the side wall and pulled herself out of the bath. With a sudden movement she felt the rigid fingers slip from her shoulders and release her.

"My God, bloody hell!" she screamed as she stood staring at the sloshing bath water, and she immediately knew what this incident meant without asking herself any questions. Her life was next on the list and it was certainly on borrowed time. On that thought she grabbed her dressing gown and fled to the lounge, expecting her ghostly predator to follow her. Standing in the middle of the room she confronted an eerie silence that warned her to re-consider her motives.

"Should I pack my bags and get out of town for a week, or should I move in with Julia?" she thought to herself. Her Slavic emotions got the better of her. "I'm going to raze that place to the ground and I don't care if I survive or not. I've had enough of this life anyway. I'm thirty six and I'm past it for marriage and having a family." As she raised her head and stared at herself in the wall mirror, she spat out in defiance, "It'll be tomorrow night after ten."

Chapter 20

As Trevor McDonald gave his final report on the small screen for News at Ten, Lena glanced up at her wall clock and clenched her fists so tightly that the whites of her knuckles poked through her skin tissue.

"You've got to go through with this, Lena. You can't back out of this," she whispered.

She had dressed in a pair of old tracksuit bottoms and a thick brown sweater along with her tatty old sneakers. After dropping her crucifix on her last visit, the only weapon she had this time was the grotty old petrol can from her garage.

"It should only take about fifteen minutes and it'll be all over and done," she kept thinking to herself as she locked the door behind her and very slyly began the precarious walk to Harley Meadows. Her mouth seemed to dry up as she ran her tongue around her mouth feeling all the fillings in her teeth until ten minutes later her rendezvous with her demonic opposition lay in front of her. As she went to the back of the house, she nervously tried the back door only to find that it was locked fast until she came to the kitchen window, which to her surprise had been smashed with a small hole as though a small stone had been thrown through it.

"Well, this makes breaking and entering all very easy," she thought as she put her left hand through the hole and opened the sash from the inside. Once inside she unscrewed the petrol can cap and sloshed a large puddle over the kitchen floor, which gave off a very powerful odorous smell.

"Lena!"

"What?" she replied.

She quickly turned around in terrible shock as she distinctly heard the voice of a Cockney old woman call her name. As she pursued the voice from the direction that it came, the voice repeated itself, this time from the dining room.

"No, don't go any further," she thought as she stayed on the same spot as though rooted to the ground.

From all around herself, she sloshed more and more petrol, giving the satisfaction that she was defying the entities that posed a threat. Suddenly a rough feminine London voice broke the untimely silence.

"You must be Lena."

Lena began to panic as she felt a great gust of cold air sweep past her back. As she let her left hand drop by her side, petrol began to run from the fuel can and add to the many other puddles of highly flammable liquid on the laminated floor. There across the hallway was the main bedroom where Natalie he died some three weeks before. To Lena it seemed a sanctuary to her protection and she very quickly tiptoed across to its doorway until suddenly a soft but desperate voice called from the room from the far side of the double bed.

"Lena, quickly, come in, you'll be safe in here."

It was the voice of Natalie and she recognized it immediately. As Lena stood by the window she could see a light transparent figure about five feet five inches tall in front of her and it spoke to her in a very unreal cold tone which felt almost chilling to listen to.

"You've got to leave here immediately, this is the one room where they can't touch you as this is the room where I died. I have my own armour of light."

Lena snapped back, "Like hell I will, these bastards have got to go."

The voice of Natalie replied, "No, you've got it wrong,

listen to me, you've got to go right now otherwise you will be the next victim who was naïve enough to ignore all the warning signs."

"I won't go, Natalie, I've made up my mind, I'm going to raze this fucking place to the ground."

The voice of Natalie whispered back. "You've got the rest of your life in front of you, girl. Just go home."

"No, Natalie, no!" and on this final word she turned around and ran out of the bedroom in a frenzied mood of absolute hysteria. Standing by the sofa she began to pour petrol over the bottom of the curtains and walked over to the dining room area, leaving an odorous trail of petroleum spirit behind her. As the final drop from the fuel can made contact with the carpet, she looked back to see that her vision of the lounge was one of absolute darkness, then suddenly, to her shocked dismay, a large bronze figure of a tall middle aged man appeared from through the floor followed by more figures, some mature adults wearing apparel of all different bygone years and others children as young as eight years old, all of them holding hands so that a spiritual circle was made around her in a pincer like trap. As Lena stood there totally transfixed by what she saw, she became overwhelmed by an oppressive force which began to drag her to the ground. Thrusting her right hand into her pocket she pulled out the Swan Vesta matches she had brought from her kitchen. On each occasion she dropped every match, caused by the oppressive force that defied her strength to carry out her plan to destroy the home of the Harrison family. Screaming at the top of her voice she bawled out, "Go to hell the lot of you!" *Psssshhhh* went the match on the third attempt as it finally ignited but fell to the carpet from Lena's twitching nervous grip making a proclaiming "boom" noise, rather like a gas ring that had been lit after some delay. As the ignited petrol pursued its trail all across the soaked carpet like a children's Hornby train set,

Lena was faced with all the satanic entities that were now all clear to see, their eyes given an intense glare by her defiant gesture. As all the amber flames shot upwards, the crackling sound of ignited furniture roared in response to this utterly hideous situation which left Lena convulsing with unconditional shock to the scorching, melting inferno that was way outside of her control. With the choking black fumes filling the whole home, she stumbled onto the protruding arm of the sofa, causing her coat to ignite immediately and go up in a blaze. Within seconds she became a human fireball, screaming and howling like a beast that was being barbarically tortured. As this horrific scene of fiery mayhem gripped the home of the Harrison family, the panicking neighbours immediately rang the emergency services as the sound of fire engine sirens could be heard along the A30.

"Hey, what's all the noise about, Julia?" snapped Alex as he swung his head around the bathroom door with dripping tooth paste all around his mouth.

"I hope to God it's not what I think it is," whinged Julia as she poked her head out of the lounge window to see in which direction the fire brigade were driving. "Oh no!" she howled and without a second's break was pulling on her Gola sneakers and overcoat to follow where the blue flashing lights were heading. "Where are my keys?" she growled in an abrupt fashion before tearing out of the front door like an RAF squadron scramble.

As the amber and blue flames gutted the bungalow with a deafening, crackling roar, the Surrey fire brigade blocked off and shut down the whole street as the neighbours and bystanders gathered all around the front wall, as one caught sight of a lonely slim female lying in the hallway wearing totally incinerated apparel.

"Oh look, there's somebody over there just inside the door," exclaimed a young teenage girl wearing her light blue satin dressing gown. It was Lena. She was dead. As Julia arrived, she clambered over the garden wall shouting "Lena! … Lena!" but the angry inferno beat her back until a burly fireman in full protective uniform came forward and held from making any more advancement to the flames. As the deafening mayhem gave an uncompromising roaring finale in the sinister darkness, Alex arrived at the scene. His inquisitive mind had got the better of him by pulling on his jogging bottoms and school shoes. Pushing his way to the front of the gawping crowd, Julia caught sight of him.

"Alex, come back, for God's sake don't look, it's no good!" she screamed with a shrieking voice with a broken heart. As the two of them stood there, Alex looked up at Julia and stared into her green eyes until she put her arms around him as protection from the overpowering heat.

"Hey, Joe, how long will jet two hold?" shouted a firefighter in his bright yellow fireproof suit. "Oh, about another ten minutes, Jack," he wearily replied.

"I think it's time we went home," suggested Julia with a voice succumbing to the horrific reality of the building. As the two of them turned their backs on the gutted home, they slowly walked back home arm in arm, leaving behind them the hustle and bustle of flashing lights of the emergency services and the foul overpowering smell of the Harrison family's gutted bungalow.

Two weeks after the blaze, Alex was re-united with his father in Vinnitsa, Ukraine. It seems a very tragic end that his mother and stepfather should stumble across spiritual land lines that brought them into contact with the worst of the spirit world to their own detriment. To those who feel inquisitive enough to want to contact the other side, you must be warned that you don't really know what you are tampering with, rather like a child lighting a firework at arm's length and then awaiting what the outcome will be. Will it give very colourful bright lights or an angry explosion? A warning to each and every one of you that the dead should be laid to rest and not woken or disturbed.

Post Script By the Author
A J Webb

I hope you were thrilled reading my story "Armour of Light" and that you learned some basic knowledge regarding the phenomenon of the paranormal. I'm sure that we have all heard certain ghost stories during our lives and I, myself, am certainly no exception. The book you have just read was based on a true story, which started when I bought my first home. It was build on the site of an old car mechanic's workshop premises where a spiritualist occult gang used to meet in the late sixties. It was here that they used Ouija boards and slaughtered small animals in satanic rituals and buried their remains at the rear of the building.

As a young schoolboy, I was a great cinema fan and loved to see all the various war films and furthermore I was taken with friends to visit the Imperial War Museum in Lambeth, South London. It was here at a young age that I became interested in World War II which led to close studies of the Third Reich, the National Socialist German Workers Party and the rise of its very notorious leader, a very certain Herr Adolf Hitler. It was inevitable that the Third Reich would become a very wide great interest to the younger generation as they displayed a variety of unpleasant, uncharitable characters such as Himmler, Heydrich and Eichmann, to name but a few. To those of us that have read up on these henchmen, we have not only learned that they were not only anti-Semitic, but within the Nazi party itself was an element of those who dabbled in the occult. As a teenager, myself and a regular friend at the time used to travel once a month to Kingston-upon-Thames. It was here that we used to visit a small, pokey militaria shop, "Warner's Militaria", down a long old Victorian shopping arcade. This shop was no ordinary antique shop. It was packed with a huge variety of Nazi SS uniforms, medals, caps, dress daggers etc. It was here that I remember the vast display of stock in his very busy shop window, especially the black SS officer's cap in excellent condition with the original "Totenkopf" cap badge attached to its front neatly positioned above the peak. The one thing that put me off buying this sought-after collector's item was the very obnoxious price tag of £250.00, which in 1977 was rather a small fortune. The other item that still sticks in my mind was this large jewellery box with a collection of silver and gold rings. One of these was the SS Ehrenring, called the Death's Head Ring. The design around its silver band demonstrates Himmler's interest in Germanic mysticism. The main thing that puzzled me at the time was the series of icons that were displayed very prominently amongst the decorative oak leaves. These four types of Armanen rune gave clear indication of the occult roots of National Socialism. These being the Sig, Hagel, Swastika and Double Rune, which all bear an expression of loyalty to the Schutzstaffel and orientation to occult phenomenon. The Hagel rune in particular has a very esoteric meaning, "Enclose the universe in you and you control the universe". I must admit that on one occasion I bought an SS swastika armband plus other Nazi memorabilia and actually being inside this shop made the hairs on my neck stand on end as it was full of the most demonic paraphernalia. Just inside the door was a very large glass cabinet with at least twenty Nazi dress daggers laid out from one end to the other, the most interesting one being the infamous SS dagger with the inscription "Meine Heure Est Treure", which translated into

English means "My honour is loyalty". Such an item today would most probably be worth about £1,500.00. Perhaps you are asking yourself, what does all this have in common with ghosts and spirits? As I mentioned in my book, in the spirit world, like attracts like and dark attracts dark. It is quite obvious that such an abundance of Nazi militaria in this shop would attract dark demonic spirits which would explain the rather heavy atmosphere. I have been advised by certain church ministers that they have been summonsed to people's homes to cure paranormal issues, that the core reasons for their problem is that they have filled up their home with very negative, un-Christian dark decorations. Some people have persistently played videos and CDs on the topic of the occult and by doing so, quite naively, sent invitation messages to the spirit world with rather detrimental repercussions. Some people have lived in homes where they are surrounded by dormant spirits and by accident awoken them by stimulating them by the ways that I have mentioned. The minister that carried out the exorcism on my home, for reasons I can't give out his name, but he told me a story of a middle aged couple that visited Egypt some years ago for their summer vacation. Once again, we have an example of a nation that has a history of spiritualism expressed by their ancient hieroglyphic paintings, icons etc. One night, this middle aged couple were exploring the pyramids of Giza on the outskirts of Cairo when suddenly a cluster of small blue lights circled around their heads and very quickly, in a split second, shot towards their chests and disappeared. Upon their return to their home in England, they awoke during the middle of the night to see two ancient Egyptian figures wearing typical head dress standing side by side in their bedroom.

To end my post script, I will leave you with one final scenario. Again this was a true account that happened to my parents' friends when they rented out a small Welsh cottage during the summer of 1954. The home they had rented out was typically Welsh that kept its

characteristics, especially its kitchen with its large oak dresser that reached as high as the ceiling. It all began during the second night of their stay when both of them, Molly and Bob, were lying in bed together, just relaxing after they had spent the evening at a local pub on the other side of the village. Suddenly, in the distance of he silence of the night, at the bottom of the old cobbled street, they heard a pair of old hob nailed boots walking very slowly towards their cottage. As they lay there, their eyes and ears flicked open as to who this totally unexpected person could be. To their total dismay, the footsteps, with their anti-social noise, got louder and louder, until they reached their front gate, and without any further ado, made their way up the garden path, only to continue up the hallway staircase and onto the landing. Both husband and wife lay there, totally knocked sideways, quivering with fear, as they experienced total silence as to what was going to happen next from behind their thick oak bedroom door. Two minutes later, their fear reached a climax when their attention was drawn to the far end of their bedroom by the loud raucous snoring. After about an hour, the sinister noise very slowly disappeared. Three nights later, they heard the same footsteps in the hallway and the sound and movement of somebody very drunk in the kitchen downstairs. Suddenly there was an eerie silence followed by an almighty crash as though the oak dresser had been pulled over and made a colossal impact with the hard tiled floor. Molly and Bob gradually tiptoed down the stairs to the kitchen and gradually pushed open the door which was slightly ajar, only to find that everything in the room was exactly as it was before they went to bed.

The following evening the two of them visited the pub at the at the bottom of the lane only to find they were almost the only ones in there. As they got chatting to the elderly landlord, they shared their extraordinary experiences over the past few evenings. The barman responded in a knowing, not surprised reaction and then explained that back in 1926, the owner returned home one night, very intoxicated on alcohol, and had a huge confrontation with his young wife. A bitter aggressive struggle took place between the pair of them which ended in her husband killing her and his daughter with a double barrelled shot gun and then turning the gun on himself. The cottage was well known for its haunting as every family that had stayed there always reported that they had experienced very strange goings on.

Please take my advice. Do not contact the dead as you don't know what you are playing with. Please enjoy life safely.

Lightning Source UK Ltd.
Milton Keynes UK
UKOW04f1915300715

256137UK00001B/6/P